The Observers Series

AIRCRAFT

About the Book

Observers Aircraft is the indispensable annual pocket guide to the world's latest aeroplanes and helicopters, and most recent versions of established aircraft types. This, the thirty-seventh annual edition, embraces the latest fixed-wing and variable-geometry aeroplanes and rotorcraft of twenty countries. Its scope ranges from such airliner newcomers as the Airbus A320-200, the Ilyushin Il-96 and the Tupolev Tu-204, through general aviation débutantes like the Bromon BR 2000, the LET 610 and new variants of the Citation and Learjet corporate transports, to such new military aircraft as the PZL I-22 Iryd light trainer/attack aircraft and the Chinese SH-5 amphibian. The latest available information is provided on the most recently-introduced Soviet military aircraft, such as the MiG-29 and Su-27, as well as the newest variants of established commercial transports, such as the Boeing 737-400 and 747-400, the Airbus A320-200 and the BAe 146-300. All data has been checked and revised as necessary, and more than half of the three-view silhouettes are new or have been revised.

About the Author

William Green, compiler of *Observers Aircraft* for 37 years, is internationally known for many works of aviation reference. He entered aviation journalism during the early years of World War II, subsequently serving with the RAF and resuming aviation writing more than 40 years ago, in 1947. William Green is currently managing editor of the monthly *AIR International*, one of the largest-circulation European-based aviation journals.

D0522753

The *Observer's* series was launched in 1937 with the publication of *The Observer's Book of Birds*. Today, fifty years later, paperback *Observers* continue to offer practical, useful information on a wide range of subjects, and with every book regularly revised by experts, the facts are right up-to-date. Students, amateur enthusiasts and professional organisations alike will find the latest *Observers* invaluable.

'Thick and glossy, briskly informative' – *The Guardian*

'If you are a serious spotter of any of the things the series deals with, the books must be indispensable' – *The Times Educational Supplement*

O B S E R V E R S

AIRCRAFT

William Green

With silhouettes by Dennis Punnett

1988/89 edition

FREDERICK WARNE

FREDERICK WARNE

Published by the Penguin Group
27 Wrights Lane, London W8 5TZ, England
Viking Penguin Inc., 40 West 23rd Street, New York, New York 10010, USA
Penguin Books Australia Ltd, Ringwood, Victoria, Australia
Penguin Books Canada Ltd, 2801 John Street, Markham, Ontario, Canada L3R 1B4
Penguin Books (NZ) Ltd, 182–190 Wairau Road, Auckland 10, New Zealand

Penguin Books Ltd, Registered Offices: Harmondsworth, Middlesex, England

Thirty-seventh edition 1988

Copyright © Frederick Warne & Co., 1988

ISBN 0 7232 3534 1

Typeset, printed and bound in Great Britain by William Clowes Limited

INTRODUCTION TO THE 1988 EDITION

WHEN, thirty-seven years ago, in 1952, the first annual edition of *Observers Aircraft* was compiled and published, its aim was to provide a concise pocket guide to the world's principal military and civil aircraft; in other words, those aircraft most likely to be seen by its possessors. With the passage of time and proliferation of new aircraft types, however, this aim had perforce to be discarded. As service lifespans of aircraft progressively lengthened, it became apparent that retention of emphasis on *numerical* importance negated justification for an annual publication as insufficient change took place from year to year among the types most frequently seen.

It became necessary, therefore, to 'prune' older aeroplanes and helicopters from each successive edition, despite their continued widespread service, in order to permit inclusion of their intended successors. As a result, *Observers Aircraft* underwent a progressive transformation of purpose; from a guide to what was to be *seen* in the world's skies to a modest directory of the *latest* shapes with wings or rotors, many of which would, for some time at least, be seen by singularly few.

Thus, today, unlike most contemporary source books, *Observers Aircraft* concerns itself primarily – as it has for more than three decades – with the most *recent* aircraft types under test at the end of the year preceding publication, those expected to fly during its year of currency and the latest variants of aircraft already established in production. This reiteration of the book's *raison d'être* has been prompted by increasing numbers of letters received from new purchasers of *Observers Aircraft* querying omission of aircraft types that they have seen. To such it can only be said that each year the *force majeure* of finding space for new aircraft dictates discarding – with reluctance – older aircraft featured in successive previous editions.

It is only by dint of such 'pruning' that it is possible to include in this, the 1988 edition, such aircraft expected to make their début this year as the new Soviet Ilyushin Il-96 and Tupolev Tu-204 airliners, and the radical new tilt-rotor Bell-Boeing V-22 Osprey. Other débutantes, so far as are concerned in *Observers Aircraft*, include the Polish I-22 Iryd jet trainer, China's large SH-5 military amphibian, the new -400 versions of Boeing's best-selling Models 737 and 747, the latest regional airliner 'stretch', the Franco-Italian ATR 72, new versions of the now vintage A-6 Intruder and A-7 Corsair, and such mid-life updates as the Sea Harrier FRS Mk 2.

WILLIAM GREEN

AERITALIA-AERMACCHI-EMBRAER AMX

Countries of Origin: Italy and Brazil.
Type: Single-seat battlefield support and light attack aircraft.
Power Plant: One 11,030 lb st (5 000 kgp) Rolls-Royce Spey Mk 807 turbofan.
Performance: Max speed (at 21,164 lb/9 600 kg), 568 mph (913 km/h) at 36,000 ft (10 975 m), or Mach = 0·86, 625 mph (1 005 km/h) at sea level; tactical radius (at 26,896 lb/12 200 kg with 5,996-lb/2 720-kg external load and 10 per cent reserve), 322 mls (520 km) HI-LO-HI, 230 mls (370 km) LO-LO-LO; ferry range (with two 220 Imp gal/1 000 l drop tanks), 1,840 mls (2 965 km).
Weights: Operational empty, 14,770 lb (6 700 kg); max take-off, 27,557 lb (12 500 kg).
Armament: (Italian) One 20-mm M61A1 rotary cannon or (Brazilian) two 30-mm DEFA 553 cannon, two AIM-9L Sidewinder or similar AAMs at wingtips and max external ordnance load (including AAMs) of 8,377 lb (3 800 kg).
Status: First prototype flown 15 May 1984. Further three (plus one replacement) prototypes flown in Italy and two additional prototypes flown in Brazil, first of the latter on 16 October 1985. Production of first batch of 30 (including three two-seaters) initiated in July 1986, and current planning calling for 187 and 79 for the Italian and Brazilian air forces respectively. Final assembly lines in both Italy and Brazil, with single-source component manufacture.
Notes: The AMX has been developed jointly by Aeritalia (47·1%) and Aermacchi (23·2%) in Italy, and Embraer (29·7%) in Brazil, and the first production aircraft is scheduled to fly April 1988.

AERITALIA-AERMACCHI-EMBRAER AMX

Dimensions: Span, 29 ft $1\frac{1}{2}$ in (8,87 m); length, 43 ft $4\frac{7}{8}$ in (13,23 m); height, 15 ft $0\frac{1}{4}$ in (4,58 m); wing area, 226·05 sq ft (21,00 m²).

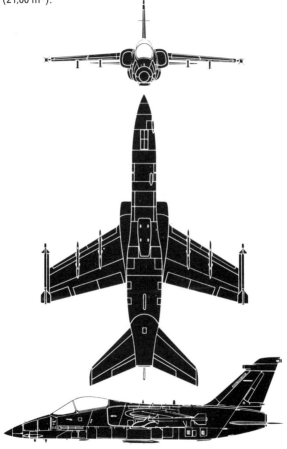

AERMACCHI MB-339C

Country of Origin: Italy.

Type: Tandem two-seat advanced trainer and light attack aircraft.

Power Plant: One 4,400 lb st (1 996 kgp) Fiat-built Rolls-Royce Viper 680-43 turbojet.

Performance: Max speed, 561 mph (902 km/h) at sea level, 518 mph (834 km/h) at 36,000 ft (10 975 m); max initial climb (50% fuel), 8,000 ft/min (40,64 m/sec); typical tactical radius (close air support with two 30-mm cannon and two LAU-51 rocket pods, and allowance for 5 min over target), 245 mls (395 km) HI-LO-HI.

Weights: Empty equipped, 7,297 lb (3 310 kg); loaded (pilot training configuration), 10,218 lb (4 635 kg); max take-off, 13,999 lb (6 350 kg).

Armament: (Training and light strike) Two 30-mm cannon in underwing pods included in max of 4,000 lb (1 815 kg) of ordnance distributed between six wing stores stations.

Status: MB-339C flown for first time on 17 December 1985 as latest development of MB-339A, the first of two prototypes of which was flown on 12 August 1976. Initial model supplied to Italian Air Force (102), Argentina (10), Dubai (five), Nigeria (12), Ghana (two), Malaysia (13) and Peru (16). Production continuing at beginning of 1988.

Notes: The MB-339C is a progressive development of the MB-339B from which it differs primarily in having a digital navigation/attack system. Whereas the MB-339A has a 4,000 lb st (1 814 kgp) Viper 632-43, the MB-339B introduced the uprated Viper 680-43. The MB-339K is a dedicated single-seat close air support version of the MB-339C with a similar Head-up Display and Nav/Attack system. A twin-engined version, the MB-339D, was being proposed at the beginning of 1988.

AERMACCHI MB-339C

Dimensions: Span (over tip tanks), 36 ft 9¾ in (11,22 m); length, 36 ft 10½ in (11,24 m); height, 12 ft 9½ in (3,90 m); wing area, 207·75 sq ft (19,30 m²).

AEROSPATIALE TB 30 EPSILON-TP

Country of Origin: France.

Type: Tandem two-seat primary/basic trainer.

Power Plant: One 360 shp Turboméca TP 319 turboprop.

Performance: Max speed, 273 mph (439 km/h) at 20,000 ft (6 095 m); max initial climb, 2,130 ft/min (10,82 m/sec).

Weights: Empty, 1,890 lb (857 kg); max take-off (aerobatic), 2,750 lb (1 247 kg).

Status: The prototype Epsilon-TP (modified prototype of the piston-engined Epsilon) was flown on 9 November 1985, and production deliveries are being offered from late 1989.

Notes: The Epsilon-TP is a turboprop-powered derivative of the current-production Epsilon, which, powered by a 300 hp Avco Lycoming AEIO-540-L1B5-D six-cylinder horizontally opposed engine, first flew on 22 December 1979. The *Armée de l'Air* possesses a total requirement for 150 Epsilons and 18 have been ordered by Portugal for assembly by OGMA at Alverca. An armed export version is being offered of which three have been delivered to Togo. This features four wing hardpoints stressed to carry 352 lb (160 kg) inboard and 176 lb (80 kg) outboard. Production rate of the Epsilon was running at two–three aircraft monthly at the beginning of 1988. The turboprop-powered Epsilon-TP does not differ fundamentally from the basic Epsilon aft of the firewall and is currently one of the lightest turbine-engined trainers on offer and closely comparable to the Valmet Redigo (see pages 212–3). The Epsilon-TP is, like its piston-engined counterpart, to be offered in armed form with a similar reinforced weapon-carrying wing. Versions were proposed with both the Allison 250 and Pratt & Whitney Canada PT6A turboprops prior to adoption of the TP 319 which has been derived from the TM 319 turboshaft.

AEROSPATIALE TB 30 EPSILON-TP

Dimensions: Span, 25 ft 11¾ in (7,92 m); length, 24 ft 10¾ in (7,59 m); height, 8 ft 8¾ in (2,66 m); wing area, 103·34 sq ft (9,60 m²).

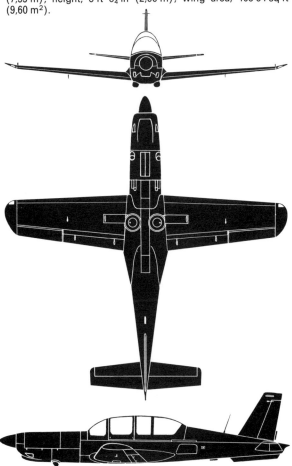

AEROSPATIALE-AERITALIA ATR 72

Countries of Origin: France and Italy.
Type: Regional commercial transport.
Power Plant: Two 2,400 shp Pratt & Whitney Canada PW124 turboprops.
Performance: (Estimated) Max cruise speed, 329 mph (530 km/h); max cruise altitude, 25,000 ft (7 620 m); range (at 47,400 lb/21 500 kg with reserves), 748 mls (1 204 km) with 16,535-lb (7 500-kg) payload, 1,727 mls (2 780 km) with 66 passengers, 2,763 mls (4 447 km) with max fuel and zero payload.
Weights: Operational empty, 26,830–26,896 lb (12 170–12 200 kg); max take-off, 44,070–47,400 lb (19 990–21 500 kg).
Accommodation: Crew of two on flight deck and optional arrangements for 64, 66, 70 or (high density) 74 passengers in four-abreast layout with central aisle.
Status: Prototype ATR 72 scheduled to enter flight test August 1988 as a stretched, more powerful derivative of the ATR 42 (see 1987 edition). Fifty-one orders and options for the ATR 72 for 13 airlines placed by 1 January 1988, at which time 120 ATR 42s had been ordered with 74 on option and 72 delivered. Combined production rate of ATR 42 and ATR 72 was four monthly at beginning of 1988 and was being increased to six monthly.
Notes: Launched in January 1986, the ATR 72 embodies a 14 ft 9 in (4,50 m) stretch by comparison with the ATR 42 giving six more seat rows. In addition, the ATR 72 has new, longer-span wings making increased use of carbonfibre. First deliveries are scheduled to Finnair in May 1989.

AEROSPATIALE-AERITALIA ATR 72

Dimensions: Span, 88 ft 9 in (27,05 m); length, 89 ft $1\frac{1}{2}$ in (27,17 m); height, 25 ft $1\frac{1}{4}$ in (7,65 m); wing area, 656·6 sq ft (61,00 m²).

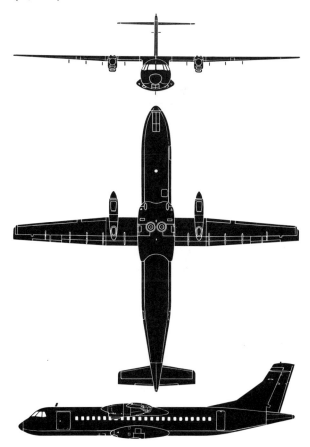

AIRBUS A300-600

Country of Origin: International consortium.
Type: Medium-haul commercial airliner.
Power Plant: Two 56,000 lb st (25 400 kgp) Pratt & Whitney JT9D-7R4H1 or General Electric CF6-80C2 turbofans.
Performance: Max cruise speed, 554 mph (891 km/h) at 31,000 ft (9 450 m); econ cruise, 536 mph (862 km/h) at 33,000 ft (10 060 m); range cruise, 518 mph (833 km/h) at 35,000 ft (10 670 m); range (max payload), 3,430 mls (5 200 km) at econ cruise, (max fuel with 52,900-lb/23 995-kg payload), 5,320 mls (8 560 km).
Weights: Operational empty, 193,410 lb (87 728 kg); max take-off, 363,760 lb (165,000 kg).
Accommodation: Flight crew of three and maximum seating for 344 passengers, a typical arrangement being for 267 passengers in a mixed-class layout.
Status: First JT9D-powered A300-600 flown on 8 July 1983, with first customer delivery (to Saudia) following in May, and first CF6-powered -600 flown on 20 March 1985. Total of 311 A300s (all versions) ordered by December 1987 when 280 delivered. Production rate (including A310) three per month at beginning of 1988.
Notes: The A300 is manufactured by a consortium of Aérospatiale (France), British Aerospace (UK), Deutsche Airbus (Federal Germany) and CASA (Spain). The A300-600 replaces the A300B4-200 (see 1983 edition) from which it differs primarily in having the new, re-profiled rear fuselage of the A310 with an extension of the parallel portion of the fuselage offering an 18-seat increase in capacity, and later-generation engines. The first CF6-80C2-powered -600 was delivered to the launch customer, Thai International, September 1985, and the extended-range A300-600R was flown 9 December 1987. The latter has 58,000 lb st (26 310 kgp) PW4158 or 60,200 lb st (27 307 kgp) CF6-80C2A3 engines.

14

AIRBUS A300-600

Dimensions: Span, 147 ft $1\frac{1}{4}$ in (44,84 m); length, 177 ft 5 in (54,08 m); height, 54 ft 3 in (16,53 m); wing area, 2,799 sq ft (260,00 m²).

AIRBUS A310-300

Country of Origin: International consortium.
Type: Medium-range commercial transport.
Power Plant: Two 50,000 lb st (22 680 kg) Pratt & Whitney JT9D-7R4E or General Electric CF6-80C2-A2 turbofans.
Performance: Max cruising speed, 561 mph (903 km/h) at 35,000 ft (10 670 m); long-range cruise, 534 mph (860 km/h) at 37,000 ft (11 280 m); range (with max payload), 4,318 mls (6 950 km) at econ cruise, (max fuel), 6,034 mls (9 710 km) at long-range cruise.
Weights: Operational empty, 169,840 lb (77 040 kg); max take-off, 330,688 lb (150 000 kg).
Accommodation: Flight crew of two or three with 280 passengers with single-class seating eight abreast, or 218 passengers in a typical mixed-class (first and economy) layout.
Status: The first A310-300 was flown on 8 July 1985, and was certified and delivered to launch customer (Swissair) in December 1985, with CF6-powered version being certified in March 1986, with service entry (by Air India) in the following June. First A310 flown on 3 April 1982, and 155 ordered by beginning of December 1987 with 110 delivered. Production rate (including A300 – see pages 14–15) three monthly.
Notes: The A310-300 differs from earlier A310 models in having an additional fuel tank in the tailplane, a carbonfibre-reinforced plastic fin, wingtip fences and a revised cockpit. By comparison with the earlier A300B, the A310 has a new, higher aspect ratio wing, a shorter fuselage, a new tailplane and a new undercarriage, but it retains a high degree of commonality with the preceding and larger aircraft. Empty weight of -300 is very similar to -200 despite higher MTOW. The Pratt & Whitney PW4152 became available as an engine option from mid-1987.

AIRBUS A310-300

Dimensions: Span, 144 ft 0 in (43.90 m); length, 153 ft 1 in (46,66 m); height, 51 ft 10 in (15,81 m); wing area, 2,357·3 sq ft (219,00 m²).

AIRBUS A320-200

Country of Origin: International consortium.
Type: Short- to medium-haul commercial transport.
Power Plant: Two 25,000 lb st (11 340 kgp) General Electric/
SNECMA CFM56-5 or IAE V2500 turbofans.
Performance: Max cruise speed, 560 mph (903 km/h) at
28,000 ft (8 535 m); range cruise, 520 mph (840 km/h) at
37,000 ft (11 280 m); range (max payload), 2,940 mls (4 730 km),
(max fuel), 4,468 mls (7 190 km).
Weights: Operational empty (typical), 86,570 lb (39 268 kg);
max take-off, 158,700 lb (71 986 kg).
Accommodation: Flight crew of two and typical mixed-class
arrangement of 12 first-class and 138 economy-class passengers, or 164 economy-class passengers.
Status: First of four flight test aircraft flown 22 February 1987,
and first for customer delivery (5th aircraft) flown 15 October
1987, with service entry (Air France) scheduled for March 1988.
Total of 309 ordered (and 174 on option) by beginning of 1988,
with production of 6·5 monthly by end of 1989 rising to 8·0
monthly mid 1990.
Notes: Initial 21 A320s are of -100 series, but 22nd and
subsequent aircraft will be of the -200 version with additional
wing centre section fuel and wingtip fences. Deliveries of the
-200 will commence September 1988, seven (including the four
flight test aircraft) flown by beginning of the year, including the
first two for Air France and the first for British Caledonian.

AIRBUS A320-200

Dimensions: Span, 111 ft 3 in (33,91 m); length, 123 ft 3 in (37,58 m); height, 38 ft 7 in (11,77 m); wing area, 1,317·5 sq ft (122,40 m²).

ANTONOV AN-32 (CLINE)

Country of Origin: USSR.

Type: Military short/medium-range transport.

Power Plant: Two 4,195 ehp Ivchenko AI-20M or 5,180 ehp AI-20DM turboprops.

Performance: (AI-20DM engines) Normal continuous cruise, 329 mph (530 km/h) at 26,250 ft (8 000 m); service ceiling, 29,525 ft (9 000 m); range with 45 min reserves (max fuel), 1,367 mls (2 200 km), (max payload), 487 mls (800 km).

Weights: (AI-20DM engines) Empty, 37,038 lb (16 800 kg); max take-off, 59,525 lb (27 000 kg).

Accommodation: Flight crew of five and 39 troops on tip-up seats along the fuselage sides, 30 fully-equipped paratroops or 24 casualty stretchers and one medical attendant. A maximum of 14,770 lb (6 700 kg) of freight may be carried.

Status: Based on the An-26 (Curl), the An-32 was first flown as a prototype late 1976, production of a more powerful version (AI-20DM engines) developed specifically for the Indian Air Force with deliveries commencing against initial order for 95 (later increased to 118) in July 1984. Some 15 An-32s have been supplied to the Peruvian Air Force and sales to Cape Verde, Sao Tome and Principe, and Tanzania have been reported.

Notes: A growth version of the An-26 intended specifically for operation under 'hot-and-high' conditions, the An-32 features automatic wing leading-edge slats, triple-slotted trailing-edge flaps, and, to compensate for the high thrust line, a full-span fixed tailplane slot. The An-32 is named Sutlej (a Punjabi river) by the Indian Air Force.

ANTONOV AN-32 (CLINE)

Dimensions: Span, 95 ft 9½ in (29,20 m); length, 77 ft 8¼ in (23,68 m); height, 28 ft 8½ in (8,75 m); wing area, 807·1 sq ft (74,98 m²).

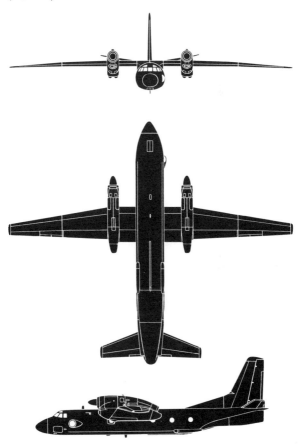

ANTONOV AN-74 (COALER-B)

Country of Origin: USSR.
Type: STOL arctic survey and support aircraft.
Power Plant: Two 14,330 lb st (6 500 kgp) Lotarev D-36 turbofans.
Performance: Max speed, 438 mph (705 km/h); normal cruise, 342 mph (550 km/h) at 26,250–32,800 ft (8 000–10 000 m); range (with 2 hrs reserves and 3,307 lb/1 500 kg freight), 2,610 mls (4 200 km); service ceiling, 32,810 ft (10 000 m).
Weights: Max take-off, 76,058 lb (34 500 kg).
Accommodation: Flight crew of four (pilot, co-pilot, navigator and engineer), stations for two hydrologists and personnel cabin with four double-seats and two bunks. Provision for up to 3,307 lb (1 500 kg) of cargo in rear portion of hold.
Status: The An-74 was first flown late 1983, with pre-series aircraft flying 1985 and full certification and series production in 1987.
Notes: The An-74 is an optimised civil version of the series An-72 (Coaler-C) STOL military tactical transport in production for and in service with the Soviet Air Force, the two being externally and dimensionally similar. The An-74 takes advantage of the 'Coanda effect' to achieve high lift, with engine exhaust gases flowing over the wing upper surfaces and inboard slotted flaps. The military An-72 was the first production transport to utilise this 'upper surface blowing', the first of the dimensionally smaller An-72 (Coaler-A) conceptual prototypes having flown on 22 December 1977. Externally, the An-72 and An-74 are virtually indistinguishable, and an airborne early warning and control system version of the former has been assigned the reporting name Madcap in the West. Madcap is unusual in that a rotodome surmounts its vertical tail surfaces.

ANTONOV AN-74 (COALER-B)

Dimensions: Span, 104 ft $7\frac{1}{2}$ in (31,89 m); length, 92 ft $1\frac{1}{4}$ in (26,07 m); height, 28 ft $4\frac{1}{2}$ in (8,65 m).

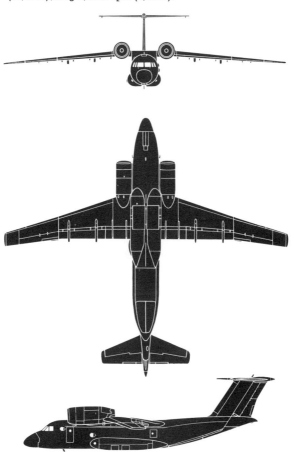

ANTONOV AN-124 RUSLAN (CONDOR)

Country of Origin: USSR.

Type: Heavy strategic freighter.

Power Plant: Four 51,650 lb st (23 430 kgp) Lotarev D-18T turbofans.

Performance: Cruising speed, 497–528 mph (800–850 km/h) at 32,810–39,370 ft (10 000–12 000 m); range (with max payload of 330,688 lb/150 000 kg), 2,796 mls (4 500 km), (max fuel), 10,250 mls (16 500 km).

Weights: Max take-off, 892,857 lb (405 000 kg).

Accommodation: Flight crew of six and upper deck seating for relief crews and up to 88 personnel. Lower deck can accommodate all elements of the SS-20 mobile intermediate-range ballistic missile system, and the largest Soviet tanks and armoured personnel carriers.

Status: First of three prototypes was flown on 26 December 1982, series production being initiated during 1984, with some 12 series aircraft delivered by beginning of 1988.

Notes: Named after a character in Russian folklore, the An-124 Ruslan is the world's largest (in terms of wing span) and heaviest aircraft, and, on 26 July 1985, established 21 international records by lifting 377,473 lb (171 219 kg) to 35,269 ft (10 750 m). Advanced features include a fly-by-wire control system, a titanium freight hold floor and extensive use of composites. The An-124 is designed for simultaneous nose and tail loading, with a visor-type lifting nose and integral forward-folding ramp. The bulk of current production is for the Soviet Air Force, replacing the An-22. The undercarriage of the An-124, each main unit of which comprises five independent twin-wheel units, permits operation from unprepared fields, hard-packed snow and ice-covered swamp.

ANTONOV AN-124 RUSLAN (CONDOR)

Dimensions: Span, 240 ft 5¾ in (73,30 m); length, 228 ft 0¼ in (69,50 m); height, 73 ft 9¾ in (22,50 m); wing area, 6,760 sq ft (628 m²).

BEECHCRAFT 1900C

Country of Origin: USA.

Type: Regional commercial, convertible passenger/freight and corporate (Exec-Liner) transport.

Power Plant: Two 1,100 shp Pratt & Whitney Canada PT6A-65B turboprops.

Performance: Max cruise speed, 295 mph (474 km/h) at 8,000 ft (2 440 m); max initial climb, 2,330 ft/min (11,84 m/sec); range (max fuel with 45 min reserves), 914 mls (1 471 km) at 25,000 ft (7 620 m), (with 'wet' wing), 1,957 mls (3 150 km).

Weights: Empty, 8,700 lb (3 947 kg); max take-off, 16,600 lb (7 530 kg).

Accommodation: Flight crew of two and standard seating (commuter) for 19 passengers in individual seats two abreast. Various corporate transport arrangements (Exec-Liner) available with typical seating from eight to 14 passengers.

Status: First of three prototypes flown on 3 September 1982, with customer deliveries commencing late 1983. More than 100 ordered by beginning of 1988, with some 80 delivered. Total of 36 aircraft scheduled to be delivered during 1988.

Notes: Offered in two basic variants as the Model 1900C with upward-hinging cargo door for regional transportation and King Air Exec-Liner for corporate transport tasks, the Beechcraft 1900 has been delivered to the Air National Guard (six) as the C-12J mission support aircraft. Some 70 Model 1900s in commuter service by beginning of 1988. Six configured for electronic surveillance missions and featuring a 'wet' wing are being supplied to the Egyptian Air Force during 1988. The Beechcraft 1900 has some 40 per cent component commonality with the King Air 200.

BEECHCRAFT 1900C

Dimensions: Span, 54 ft 6 in (16,61 m); length, 57 ft 10 in (17,63 m); height, 14 ft 10¾ in (4,53 m); wing area, 303 sq ft (28,15 m²).

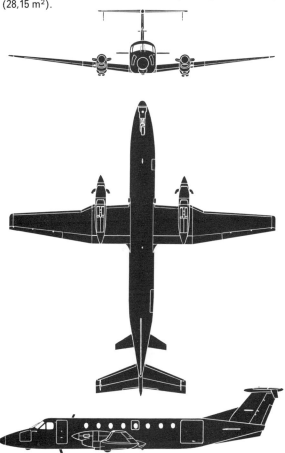

BEECHCRAFT 400 BEECHJET

Country of Origin: USA (Japan).
Type: Light corporate executive transport.
Power Plant: Two 2,900 lb st (1 315 kgp) Pratt & Whitney Canada JT15D-5 turbofans.
Performance: Max Speed, 520 mph (837 km/h), or Mach = 0·785; typical speed at 39,000 ft (11 890 m), 465 mph (748 km/h); initial climb, 3,960 ft/min (20,12 m/sec); ceiling, 41,000 ft (12 495 m); max range (with four passengers and IFR reserves), 1,760 mls (2 832 km), (with VFR reserves), 2,220 mls (3 572 km).
Weights: Basic operational, 9,315 lb (4 225 kg); max take-off, 15,780 lb (7 158 kg).
Accommodation: Pilot and co-pilot on flight deck and standard arrangement in main cabin for eight passengers, with five individual seats and a three-place sofa. Optional nine-seat arrangement.
Status: The Beechjet is a derivative of the Mitsubishi Diamond 2, the manufacturing rights in which have been acquired from the Japanese company by the Beech Aircraft Corporation. Four of five Diamond 2s acquired by Beech were modified as Beechjets during 1986, and the first Beech-assembled aircraft was completed in August of that year, with 29 delivered by the end of 1987. Production was continuing at 1·5 aircraft monthly at the beginning of 1988.
Notes: The Beechjet is basically a re-engined version of the Mitsubishi Diamond 2 embodying a new interior and various refinements. A progressive development of the Diamond 1 and 1A, the Diamond 2 was first flown on 20 June 1984, the first production aircraft flying on 28 January 1985. Eleven were produced by Mitsubishi of which six were sold, the remainder being acquired by Beech. The 1988 production version offers EFIS (Electronic Flight Instrumentation System), certification for an eighth seat as standard and enlarged baggage area.

BEECHCRAFT 400 BEECHJET

Dimensions: Span, 43 ft 6 in (13,25 m); length, 48 ft 5 in (14,75 m); height, 13 ft 9 in (4,19 m); wing area, 241·4 sq ft (22,43 m²).

BEECHCRAFT 2000 STARSHIP 1

Country of Origin: USA.

Type: Light corporate executive transport.

Power Plant: Two 1,100 shp Pratt & Whitney Canada PT6A-67 turboprops.

Performance: Max cruise speed, 405 mph (652 km/h) at 25,000 ft (7 620 m); econ cruise, 313 mph (504 km/h) at 39,000 ft (11 885 m); max initial climb, 3,248 ft/min (16,50 m/sec); certified ceiling, 41,000 ft (12 495 m); max fuel range (45 min reserves), 2,294 mls (3 691 km) at max cruise power, (max payload with 45 min reserves), 1,298 mls (2 089 km).

Weights: Empty equipped, 8,916 lb (4 044 kg); max take-off, 14,000 (6 350 kg).

Accommodation: Provision for two crew on flight deck and max of 10 passengers in main cabin. Six basic interior configurations offered, a typical arrangement providing seven single seats and a two-place divan.

Status: First of three prototypes of the Starship flown on 15 February 1986, this being preceded (on 29 August 1983) by an 85 per cent scale proof-of-concept vehicle. Certification was scheduled for spring of 1988, with customer deliveries expected to begin in the last quarter of 1988. Orders for more than 60 placed by beginning of 1988.

Notes: The Starship is innovative in concept in that it mates an aft-mounted laminar-flow wing with a variable-sweep foreplane, the sweep being changed with flap extension to provide fully-automatic pitch-trim compensation. Extensive use is made in the structure of such materials as boron, carbon, Kevlar and glassfibre, but the incorporation of design changes has resulted in empty weight growth and a 15-month delay in certification and initial customer deliveries.

BEECHCRAFT 2000 STARSHIP 1

Dimensions: Span, 54 ft 0 in (16,46 m); length, 46 ft 1 in (14,05 m); height, 12 ft 10 in (3,91 m); wing area, 280·9 sq ft (26,09 m²).

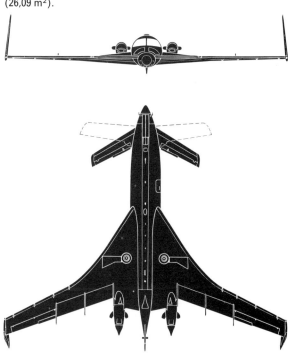

BELL-BOEING V-22 OSPREY

Country of Origin: USA.
Type: Multi-mission tilt-rotor aircraft.
Power Plant: Two 6,150 shp Allison T406-AD-400 turboshafts.
Performance: Max speed, 345 mph (556 km/h); max cruise, 317 mph (510 km/h) at sea level; range (MV-22A), 460 mls (740 km) STO at 60,500 lb (27 443 kg), 690 mls (1 110 km) STO at 55,000 lb (24 948 kg); max ferry range, 2,420 mls (3 890 km); time on station (HV-22A), 3·7 hrs VTO at 48,403 lb (21 956 kg) at radius of 250 mls (402 km).
Weights: Empty, 31,772 lb (14 412 kg); max take-off (VTO), 47,500 lb (21 546 kg), (STO) 55,000 lb (24 948 kg), self-deployment STO, 60,500 lb (27 443 kg).
Accommodation: Crew of three and (MV-22A) 24 troops or external load of 10,000 lb (4 536 kg), (CV-22A) 12 special forces troops.
Status: First of six flying prototypes scheduled to enter test June 1988. US Marine Corps has requirement for 552 assault transports (MV-22A), US Navy has requirement for up to 50 combat search and rescue aircraft (HV-22A), USAF requires 80 special operations aircraft (CV-22A) and US Army plans to procure 231 multi-mission transports. Production deliveries scheduled to begin December 1991.
Notes: Being developed jointly by Bell and Boeing, the Osprey will be capable of short or vertical take-offs and will feature folding wing and rotor systems. A pre-design study of an anti-submarine warfare version (SV-22) had begun by the beginning of 1988, when concept studies for possible commercial versions (36–44 passengers) were also in progress.

Dimensions: Span (over rotors), 84 ft 8¾ in (25,77 m); length (excluding probe), 57 ft 4 in (17,47 m).

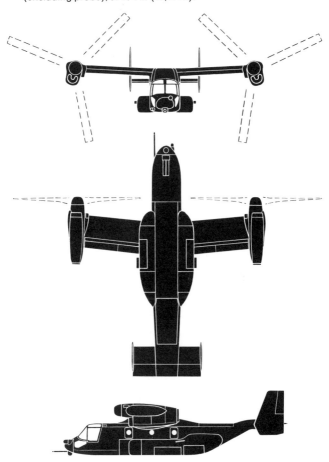

BOEING 737-400

Country of Origin: USA.
Type: Short-haul commercial transport.
Power Plant: Two 22,000 lb st (9 980 kgp) General Electric CFM56-3B-2 or 23,500 lb st (10 660 kgp) CFM56-3C turbofans.
Performance: (CFM56-3B-2) Max cruise speed (at 122,000 lb/55 339 kg), 567 mph (912 km/h); econ cruise, 483 mph (778 km/h) at 35,000 ft (10 670 m); range (max payload), 2,244 mls (3 610 km), (max fuel), 3,257 mls (5 240 km).
Weights: Operational empty, 73,790 lb (33 471 kg); max take-off, 138,500 lb (62 824 kg).
Accommodation: Flight crew of two and typical mixed-class arrangement for 146 passengers, with maximum of 168 passengers.
Status: First 737-400 was rolled out on 26 January 1988, with customer deliveries (to Piedmont) scheduled to commence September 1988. A total of 1,925 Model 737s (all versions) had been ordered by the beginning of 1988 (including 66 -500s) when production rate was 14 aircraft monthly.
Notes: The latest version of the basic Boeing 737, which has sold in greater numbers than any other airliner, the -400 offers upgraded technology by comparison with the -300 (see 1987 edition) and embodies a fuselage stretch comprising two 'plugs', one of 5 ft 6 in (1,68 m) forward of the wing and the other of 4 ft 0 in (1,22 m) aft of the wing. The outer wings and undercarriage have been strengthened to permit increased landing weights. Take-off weights of up to 142,000 lb (64 410 kg) will be available on later -400 series aircraft and it is claimed that, in 156-seat all-economy layout, the seat-mile costs are seven per cent better than those of the -300. The 737-500 is a 'short fuselage' version for 100–120 passengers which is due to be certificated in February 1990.

Dimensions: Span, 94 ft 9 in (28,90 m); length, 119 ft 1 in (36,30 m); height, 36 ft 6 in (11,12 m); wing area, 980 sq ft (91,04 m²).

BOEING 747-400

Country of Origin: USA.

Type: Long-haul commercial transport.

Power Plant: (Options) Four 57,900 lb st (26 263 kgp) General Electric CF6-80C2, 56,750 lb st (25 742 kgp) Pratt & Whitney PW4256, or 58,000 lb st (26 309 kgp) Rolls-Royce RB.211-524D4D turbofans.

Performance: (CF6-80C2) Max cruise speed, 583 mph (939 km/h) at 35,000 ft (10 670 m); econ cruise, 564 mph (907 km/h); range (max payload), 7,940 mls (12 780 km), (max fuel), 9,445 mls (15 200 km).

Weights: Operational empty (412 passengers and tri-class interior), 391,200 lb (177 450 kg); max take-off, 870,000 lb (394 630 kg).

Accommodation: Flight crew of two and typical three-class seating for 450 passengers, with max of 660 passengers.

Status: First 747-400 rolled out on 26 January 1988 and was scheduled to fly in March, with certification and first delivery planned for last quarter of year. Production rate (all 747 models) of 2·5 monthly, with some 834 ordered by beginning of 1988, including a 100 747-400s.

Notes: The 747-400 differs in a number of respects from the -300 (see 1987 edition), the most significant external difference being an extended wing with vertical winglets. Incorporating a two-crew flight deck and a flight crew rest area, the -400 offers a 13–15 per cent reduction in fuel burn per passenger seat compared with the -300. The engine nacelles have been retailored and their struts redesigned, and a new interior offers more stowage space, although the fuselage dimensions remain unchanged. The first example has Pratt & Whitney engines, the second (April) has General Electric engines and the third (June) has Rolls-Royce engines.

Dimensions: Span, 212 ft 2 in (64,67 m); length, 231 ft 10$\frac{1}{4}$ in (70,67 m); height, 63 ft 4 in (19,30 m); wing area (reference), 5,650 sq ft (524,88 m²).

BOEING 757-200

Country of Origin: USA.

Type: Short/medium-haul commercial airliner.

Power Plant: Two 37,500 lb st (17 010 kgp) Rolls-Royce RB.211-535C, 38,200 lb st (17 327 kgp) Pratt & Whitney 2037 or 40,100 lb st (18 190 kgp) Rolls-Royce RB.211-535E4 turbofans.

Performance: (RB.211-535E engines) Max cruise speed, 570 mph (917 km/h) at 30,000 ft (9 145 m); econ cruise, 528 mph (850 km/h) at 39,000 ft (11 885 m); range (max payload), 2,210 mls (3 556 km) at econ cruise, (max fuel), 5,343 mls (8 598 km) at long-range cruise.

Weights: Operational empty, 128,450 lb (58 265 kg); max take-off (RB.211-535E engines), 220,000 lb (99 790 kg).

Accommodation: Flight crew of two (with provision for optional third crew member) and typical arrangement of 178 mixed class or 196 tourist class passengers, with max single-class seating for 239 passengers.

Status: First Model 757 flown on 19 February 1982, with first customer deliveries (to Eastern) December 1982 and (British Airways) January 1983. Orders totalling 239 aircraft by January 1988, with deliveries with Pratt & Whitney engines having commenced (to Delta Air Lines) October 1984. Production rate of four aircraft monthly at beginning of 1988, with total of 151 delivered.

Notes: Two versions of the Model 757 are currently on offer, one with a max take-off weight of 220,000 lb (99 790 kg) and the other with a max take-off weight of 240,000 lb (108 864 kg). At the beginning of 1988, Boeing was offering the extended-range 757ER (deliveries of which commenced in May 1986), the 757PF freighter and the Model 757-200 Combi, with options of 230,000 lb (104,328 kg) and 240,000 lb (108 864 kg) in max take-off weights.

Dimensions: Span, 124 ft 6 in (37,82 m); length, 155 ft 3 in (47,47 m); height, 44 ft 6 in (13,56 m); wing area, 1,951 sq ft (181,25 m²).

BOEING 767-300

Country of Origin: USA.

Type: Medium-haul commercial airliner.

Power Plant: Two 50,000 lb st (22 680 kgp) Pratt & Whitney JT9D-7R4E or General Electric CF6-80A2 turbofans.

Performance: (CF6-80A2 engines) Max cruise speed, 557 mph (897 km/h) at 39,000 ft (11 890 m); econ cruise, 528 mph (850 km/h) at 39,000 ft (11 890 m); range (with max payload), 3,520 mls (5 665 km) at econ cruise, (max fuel), 5,780 mls (9 305 km) at long-range cruise.

Weights: (CF6-80A-2 engines) Operational empty, 187,900 lb (85 231 kg); max take-off, 351,000 lb (159 213 kg).

Accommodation: Flight crew of two and typical mixed-class seating for 24 first-class passengers six-abreast and 237 tourist-class passengers seven-abreast with two aisles.

Status: First Model 767 flown on 26 September 1981, with first customer delivery (to United) on 18 August 1982. First -300 flown on 1 February 1986, and first customer delivery (to Japan Air Lines) on 25 September 1986. Total of 268 (all models) ordered by January 1988 with some 188 delivered.

Notes: The -300 version of the Model 767 differs from the -200 (see 1986 edition) in embodying a 21·25-ft (6,48-m) fuselage stretch. Under offer are the -300ER (Extended Range) and -300LR (Long Range) versions. The former, deliveries of which began in February 1988, has a gross weight of 407,000 lb (184 615 kg), with 60,000 lb st (27 216 kgp) PW 4060 61,500 lb st (27 896 kgp) CF6-80C2 or 60,600 lb st (27 488 kgp) RB.211-524D4D engines. At the beginning of 1988, a -400 version with an additional fuselage stretch of approx 10 ft (3,00 m) and providing about 28 more seats was under consideration, this having a range of 5,295–5,990 mls (8 520–9 640 km).

BOEING 767-300

Dimensions: Span, 156 ft 1 in (47,60 m); length, 180 ft 3 in (54,94 m); height, 52 ft 0 in (15,85 m); wing area, 3,050 sq ft (283,3 m²).

BOEING E-3 SENTRY

Country of Origin: USA.

Type: Airborne warning and control system aircraft.

Power Plant: Four 21,000 lb st (9 525 kgp) Pratt & Whitney TF33-PW-100A turbofans.

Performance: (At max weight) Average cruise speed, 479 mph (771 km/h) at 28,900–40,100 ft (8 810–12 220 m); average loiter speed, 376 mph (605 km/h) at 29,000 ft (8 840 m); time on station (unrefuelled) at 1,150 mls (1 850 km) from base, 6 hrs, (with one refuelling), 14·4 hrs; ferry range, 5,034 mls (8 100 km) at 475 mph (764 km/h).

Weights: Empty, 170,277 lb (77 238 kg); normal loaded, 214,300 lb (97 206 kg); max take-off, 325,000 lb (147 420 kg).

Accommodation: Operational crew of 17 comprising flight crew of four, systems maintenance team of four, a battle commander and an air defence team of eight.

Status: First of two (EC-137D) development aircraft flown 9 February 1972, two pre-production E-3As following in 1975. First 24 delivered to USAF as E-3As have been modified to E-3B standards, and final 10 (including updated third test aircraft) were delivered as E-3Cs. Eighteen were delivered (in similar configuration to E-3C) to NATO as E-3As with completion April 1985. Five CFM56-powered aircraft supplied to Saudi Arabia between August 1985 and March 1987, and seven to be supplied to the RAF and four (plus two on option) to the *Armée de l'Air* in 1991.

Notes: Aircraft initially delivered to USAF as E-3As have now been fitted with JTIDS (Joint Tactical Information Distribution System), ECM-resistant voice communications, additional HF and UHF radios, austere maritime surveillance capability and more situation display consoles as E-3Bs. The E-3C featured most E-3B modifications at the production stage. The CFM-engined E-3s to be supplied to the UK and France will be equipped for flight refuelling.

BOEING E-3 SENTRY

Dimensions: Span, 145 ft 9 in (44,42 m); length, 152 ft 11 in (46,61 m); height, 42 ft 5 in (12,93 m); wing area, 2,892 sq ft (268,67 m²).

BRITISH AEROSPACE 125-800

Country of Origin: United Kingdom.

Type: Light corporate executive transport.

Power Plant: Two 4,300 lb st (1 950 kgp) Garrett TFE371-5R-1H turbofans.

Performance: Max cruise speed, 525 mph (845 km/h) at 29,000 ft (8 840 m); econ cruise, 461 mph (741 km/h) at 39,000–43,000 ft (11 900–13 100 m); max initial climb, 3,100 ft/min (15,75 m/sec); service ceiling, 43,000 ft (13 100 m); range (max payload), 3,305 mls (5 318 km), (max fuel with VFR reserves), 3,454 mls (5 560 km).

Weights: Typical operational empty, 15,120 lb (6 858 kg); max take-off, 27,400 lb (12 430 kg).

Accommodation: Flight crew of two (with provision for third crew member on flight deck) and standard arrangement for eight passengers in main cabin, with optional arrangements for up to 14 passengers.

Status: Prototype of Series 800 BAe 125 flown on 26 May 1983, with initial customer deliveries commencing in the following year. Production rate of two aircraft monthly during 1987, with sales of Series 800 totalling 108 by beginning of 1988.

Notes: The BAe 125-800 is an extensively revised development of the Series 700 (see 1982 edition) with more powerful engines, new, longer-span outboard wing sections, new ailerons, redesigned flight deck and larger ventral fuel tank. Sales of earlier turbojet- and turbofan-powered models of the BAe 125 totalled 573 aircraft, including 215 of the Series 700 aircraft. The BAe 125 serves in crew training, aeromedical and airways calibration roles as well as that of corporate transport.

BRITISH AEROSPACE 125-800

Dimensions: Span, 51 ft 4½ in (15,66 m); length, 51 ft 2 in (15,59 m); height, 17 ft 7 in (5,37 m); wing area, 374 sq ft (32,75 m²).

BRITISH AEROSPACE 146-300

Country of Origin: United Kingdom.
Type: Short-haul regional airliner.
Power Plant: Four 6,970 lb st (3 161 kgp) Textron Lycoming ALF 502R-5 turbofans.
Performance: Max cruise, 487 mph (784 km/h) at 24,000 ft (7 315 m); econ cruise, 439 mph (706 km/h) at 31,000 ft (9 450 m); range (max payload of 23,500 lb/10 660 kg), 1,588 mls (2 556 km), (optional fuel and 18,446-lb/8 367-kg payload), 2,154 mls (3 467 km).
Weights: Operational empty (typical), 54,000 lb (24 494 kg); max take-off, 95,000 lb (43 092 kg).
Accommodation: Flight crew of two and 110 passengers six abreast or 100 passengers five abreast, with optional mixed class arrangements (eg, 35 business and 65 economy class passengers, or 10 first class and 84 economy class).
Status: Aerodynamic prototype (conversion of Srs 100 prototype) flown on 1 May 1987, with first customer deliveries (to Air Wisconsin) scheduled for last quarter of 1988. Orders for all versions of the BAe 146 totalled 109 aircraft at beginning of January 1988 when some 90 delivered and production rate rising from two to 3.3 monthly.
Notes: The 146-300 differs from the -200 primarily in having a 7 ft 10 in (2,39 m) fuselage stretch. The 146-200 is available in QT (Quiet Trader) freighter version with a strengthened floor and freight door, and a QT version of the 146-300 was under study at the beginning of 1988.

BRITISH AEROSPACE 146-300

Dimensions: Span, 86 ft 5 in (26,34 m); length, 101 ft 8 in (30,99 m); height, 28 ft 3 in (8,61 m); wing area, 832 sq ft (77,30 m²).

BRITISH AEROSPACE ATP

Country of Origin: United Kingdom.
Type: Regional commercial transport.
Power Plant: Two 2,150 shp (2,400 shp emergency) Pratt & Whitney Canada PW124A or 2,653 shp PW126 turboprops.
Performance: Max cruise speed, 306 mph (492 km/h) at 15,000 ft (4 670 m); econ cruise, 301 mph (485 km/h) at 18,000 ft (5 485 m); typical initial climb, 1,370 ft/min (6,96 m/sec); range (with max payload of 14,830 lb/6 727 kg), 662 mls (1 065 km), (with 64 passengers), 1,134 mls (1 825 km), (max fuel and 8,000-lb/3 629-kg payload), 2,140 mls.
Weights: Operational empty (typical), 29,970 lb (13 594 kg); max take-off, 49,500 lb (22 453 kg).
Accommodation: Flight crew of two and standard arrangement for 64 passengers four abreast, with optional high-density arrangement for 72 passengers.
Status: First of two prototypes flown on 6 August 1986, followed by second on 20 February 1987. Certification was scheduled for January 1988 when firm orders and options totalled 24 aircraft. A production tempo of 18 aircraft annually is expected to be attained before the end of 1989, and BAe had committed 45 ATPs to production by January 1988. The initial delivery (to British Midland) was scheduled for March 1988.
Notes: Technically a stretched development of the BAe 748, its designation signifying 'Advanced TurboProp', the ATP utilises new engines, systems and equipment, swept vertical tail surfaces and a redesigned fuselage nose. It also incorporates an advanced flight deck embodying an electronic flight instrument system (EFIS) and is claimed to be the only new-generation regional turboprop capable of utilising jetways at major airports. ATPs to be delivered to Wings West from June 1988 are configured for 68 passengers.

BRITISH AEROSPACE ATP

Dimensions: Span, 100 ft 6 in (30,63 m); length, 85 ft 4 in (26,01 m); height, 23 ft 5 in (7,14 m); wing area, 842·84 sq ft (78,30 m²).

BRITISH AEROSPACE EAP

Country of Origin: United Kingdom.
Type: Single-seat advanced fighter technology demonstrator.
Power Plant: Two (approx) 9,000 lb st (4 082 kgp) dry and 16,500 lb st (7 484 kgp) reheat Turbo-Union RB199-34R Mk 104D turbofans.
Performance: No details have been released for publication but it is assumed that max speed exceeds 1,320 mph (2 124 km/h), or Mach = 2·0, above 36,000 ft (10 975 m).
Weights: Empty (approx), 22,050 lb (10 000 kg); loaded (clean), (approx) 32,000 lb (14 515 kg).
Armament: (Typical) Four BAe Sky Flash (two beneath fuselage and two beneath wing roots) and two AIM-9L Sidewinders (at wingtips) AAMs
Status: Single example flown for first time on 8 August 1986.
Notes: The EAP (Experimental Aircraft Programme) technology demonstrator is intended to investigate high AOA (Angle of Attack) operation and other flight characteristics demanded of the next generation of fighters, and various basic new technologies. These include advanced structural design with extensive use of carbonfibre composites, active fly-by-wire controls and an advanced electronic cockpit. The EAP is providing data for the EFA (European Fighter Aircraft) being developed by Eurofighter GmbH (formed by the UK, Germany, Italy and Spain). The EFA is of fundamentally similar configuration to that of the EAP, but smaller and lighter, with a basic mass empty weight of 20,945 lb (9 500 kg) and a 53-deg delta wing of 34·45 ft (10,50 m) span and 538·2 sq ft (50,00 m^2) area. The EAP is not intended for weapons systems demonstration, but makes provision for the carriage of missiles as described above.

BRITISH AEROSPACE EAP

Dimensions: Span, 36 ft 7¾ in (11,17 m); length (over probe), 48 ft 2¾ in (14,70 m); height, 18 ft 1⅜ in (5,52 m); wing area, 560 sq ft (52,00 m²).

BRITISH AEROSPACE HARRIER GR MK 5

Countries of Origin: United Kingdom and USA.
Type: Single-seat V/STOL close support and tactical reconnaissance aircraft.
Power Plant: One (short lift wet) 21,180 lb st (9 607 kgp) and (combat) 18,750 lb st (8 505 kgp) Rolls-Royce Pegasus Mk 105 vectored-thrust turbofan.
Performance: Max speed (clean), 647 mph (1 041 km/h) at sea level, or Mach=0·85, 600 mph (966 km/h) at 36,000 ft, or Mach=0·91; tactical radius (interdiction with seven Mk 82 bombs, 25-mm cannon and two 250 Imp gal/1 136 l drop tanks), 553 mls (889 km) HI-LO-HI; ferry range (with four 250 Imp gal/ 1 136 l external tanks), 2,440 mls (3 927 km).
Weights: Operational empty, 13,798 lb (6 258 kg); max take-off VTO (ISA), 18,950 lb (8 595 kg), STO, 29,750 lb (13 495 kg).
Armament: Two 25-mm cannon (on under-fuselage stations) and up to 16 Mk 82 or six Mk 83 bombs, six BL-755 cluster bombs, four Maverick ASMs, or ten rocket pods on six wing stations. Max external load, 9,200 lb (4 173 kg).
Status: First of two (weapon system) development aircraft flown on 30 April 1985, with deliveries to RAF against initial order for 60 series aircraft commencing in 1987, and service entry on 1 July of that year. Long lead items ordered for further 27 aircraft by late 1986.
Notes: The Harrier GR Mk 5 is the RAF equivalent of the US Marine Corps' AV-8B Harrier II, airframe production being divided between British Aerospace and McDonnell Douglas. Night-capable aircraft available from 1990 will be designated GR Mk 7. The prototype night attack version of the AV-8B was first flown on 26 June 1987. The USMC has a requirement for 328 AV-8Bs of which 28 are being supplied as tandem two-seat TAV-8Bs (see pages 158–9) for instructional purposes. Twelve were delivered to the Spanish Navy (as EAV-8Bs) from October 1987. The AV-8B version carries a single five-barrel 25-mm cannon.

BRITISH AEROSPACE HARRIER GR MK 5

Dimensions: Span, 30 ft 4 in (9,24 m); length, 46 ft 4 in (14,12 m); height, 11 ft 7$\frac{3}{4}$ in (3,55 m); wing area, 230 sq ft (21,37 m^2).

BRITISH AEROSPACE HAWK 100

Country of Origin: United Kingdom.

Type: Tandem two-seat advanced systems trainer and light attack aircraft.

Power Plant: One 5,845 lb st (2 650 kgp) Rolls-Royce Turboméca Adour 871 turbofan.

Performance: Max speed, 644 mph (1 037 km/h) at sea level; econ cruise, 495 mph (796 km/h) at 41,000 ft (12 500 m); combat radius (HI-LO-HI), 760 mls (1 223 km) with two 1,000-lb (453,6-kg) bombs, 316 mls (509 km) with seven 1,000-lb (453,6-kg) bombs.

Weights: Empty, 8,500 lb (3 855 kg); max take-off, 18,890 lb (8 570 kg).

Armament: Max external ordnance load of 7,200 lb (3 265 kg) on five external pylons.

Status: The aerodynamic prototype of the Hawk 100 (modified from manufacturer's Hawk 60 demonstrator) flown in October 1987.

Notes: The Hawk 100 is an enhanced development of the Hawk basic/advanced trainer (see 1985 edition and front cover) sharing with the single-seat Hawk 200 (see pages 56–57) the Adour 871 which replaces the 5,200 lb st (2 359 kgp) Adour 151 of the RAF's Hawk T Mk 1, and the 5,340 lb st (2 422 kgp) Adour 851 and 5,700 lb st (2 585 kgp) Adour 861 of the export Hawk 50 and 60 respectively. The Hawk 100 differs externally from previous two-seat versions of the aircraft primarily in having an extended nose accommodating a laser ranger, forward-looking infrared and a nav/attack avionics. This nose is an option on the single-seat Hawk 200. The Hawk 100 features an advanced head-up display/weapons aiming computer, advanced cockpit displays and provision for carrying an ECM pod. (See T-45A Goshawk, pages 154–5).

BRITISH AEROSPACE HAWK 100

Dimensions: Span, 30 ft 9¾ in (9,39 m); length, 39 ft 6 in (12,04 m); height, 13 ft 8 in (4,15 m); wing area, 179·64 sq ft (16,69 m²).

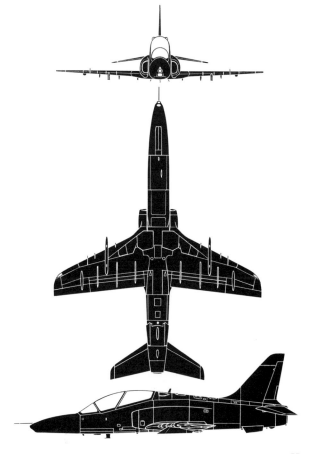

BRITISH AEROSPACE HAWK 200

Country of Origin: United Kingdom.
Type: Single-seat multi-role fighter.
Power Plant: One 5,845 lb st (2 650 kgp) Rolls-Royce Turboméca Adour 871 turbofan.
Performance: Max speed, 645 mph (1 037 km/h) at 8,000 ft (2 440 m), or Mach = 0·87; service ceiling, 50,000 ft (15 240 m); tactical radius (LO-LO close air support), 200 mls (322 km) with eight 500-lb/227-kg bombs, 120 mls (193 km) with five 1,000-lb/454-kg and four 500-lb/227-kg bombs, (HI-LO-HI interdiction), 667 mls (1 073 km) with 3,000-lb (1 360-kg) warload; ferry range (with two 190 Imp gal/860 l and one 130 Imp gal/590 l tanks), 2,240 mls (3 606 km).
Weights: Empty, 9,100 lb (4 127 kg); max take-off, 19,000 lb (8 618 kg).
Armament: Two 25-mm Aden or 27-mm Mauser cannon and max external warload of 7,700 lb (3 493 kg) on centreline and four wing stations.
Status: First prototype flown on 19 May 1986 with first pre-production aircraft flown on 24 April 1987.
Notes: The Hawk 200 is a dedicated single-seat combat derivative of the two-seat Hawk basic/advanced trainer and light tactical aircraft (see pages 54–55), sharing with the two-seat Hawk 100 the Adour 871. Roles envisaged include airspace denial, close support, battlefield support and anti-shipping strike. The Hawk 200 retains some 80 per cent commonality with the Hawk 100 with which it shares an inertial navigator, head-up display, laser rangefinder and weapon aiming computer. A multi-mode radar may be fitted in conjunction with advanced weapons (e.g., Sea Eagle).

BRITISH AEROSPACE HAWK 200

Dimensions: Span, 30 ft 9¾ in (9,39 m); length, 37 ft 4 in (11,30 m); height, 13 ft 8 in (4,15 m); wing area, 179·64 sq ft (16,69 m²).

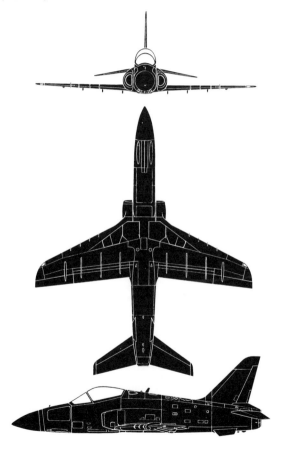

BRITISH AEROSPACE JETSTREAM 31

Country of Origin: United Kingdom.
Type: Light regional airliner and corporate transport.
Power Plant: Two 940 shp Garrett TPE331-10 turboprops.
Performance: Max cruise speed, 299 mph (482 km/h) at 20,000 ft (6 100 m); long-range cruise, 265 mph (426 km/h) at 25,000 ft (7 620 m); initial climb, 2,200 ft/min (11,2 m/sec); max range (with 19 passengers and IFR reserves), 737 mls (1 186 km), (with 12 passengers), 1,094 mls (1 760 km), (with nine passengers), 1,324 mls (2 130 km).
Weights: Operational empty, 9,613 lb (4 360 kg); max take-off, 15,322 lb (6 950 kg).
Accommodation: Flight crew of two and commuter airliner arrangement for 18–19 passengers three abreast, or basic corporate executive seating for eight passengers and optional 12-seat executive shuttle arrangement.
Status: First Jetstream 31 flown on 18 March 1982, following flight development aircraft (converted from Series 1 airframe) flown on 28 March 1980. First customer delivery (Contactair) made 15 December 1982, and 200 aircraft sold (with 70 options) by beginning of 1988, when production tempo was four aircraft monthly, and 171 had been delivered to 28 operators.
Notes: The Jetstream 31 is a derivative of the Handley Page H.P.137 Jetstream, the original prototype of which was flown on 18 August 1967. Apart from four aircraft for Royal Navy observer training with ASR 360 radar (Jetstream T Mk 3s) and two systems training versions supplied to Saudi Arabia (illustrated above), all aircraft of this type so far sold have been of the basic 'Commuter' configuration. An enhanced performance version, the Super 31 with 1,020 shp TPE331-12 engines, was introduced mid 1987.

BRITISH AEROSPACE JETSTREAM 31

Dimensions: Span, 52 ft 0 in (15,85 m); length, 47 ft 2 in (14,37 m); height, 17 ft 6 in (5,37 m); wing area, 270 sq ft (25,08 m²).

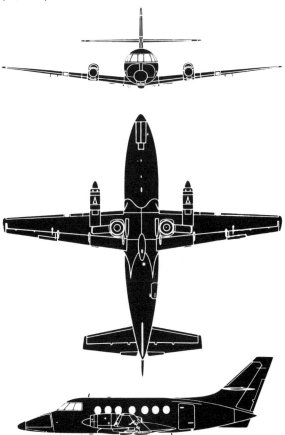

BRITISH AEROSPACE SEA HARRIER FRS MK 2

Country of Origin: United Kingdom.

Type: Single-seat V/STOL shipboard multirole fighter.

Power Plant: One 21,500 lb st (9 760 kgp) Rolls-Royce Pegasus 104 vectored-thrust turbofan.

Performance: Max speed, 720 mph (1 160 km/h) at 1,000 ft (305 m); or Mach=0·95, 607 mph (977 km/h) at 36,000 ft (10 975 m), or Mach=0·92, (with two each Martel ASMs and AIM-9L AAMs), 598 mph (962 km/h) at sea level, or Mach=0·83; combat radius (high-altitude intercept with 3 min combat), 460 mls (750 km), (strike), 288 mls (463 km).

Weights: Approx operational empty, 14,500 lb (6 577 kg); max take-off, 26,500 lb (12 020 kg).

Armament: External fuselage packs for two 25-mm or 30-mm cannon, or two AIM-120 AAM pylons on fuselage stations, plus two stores stations under each wing for free-fall or retarded 1,000-lb (453,6-kg) bombs, cluster bombs, Matra 115/116 68-mm rocket packs, AIM-9L, AIM-120 or Magic AAMs, Sea Eagle ASMs, etc.

Status: First of two development FRS Mk 2s expected to enter flight test summer 1988, with 40 FRS Mk 1 aircraft to be rotated through mid-lift update programme to FRS Mk 2 standard during 1991–4.

Notes: To enter service in 1989, the Sea Harrier FRS Mk 2 will be able to engage multiple low-flying targets beyond visual range, will have a Blue Vixen pulse-Doppler radar and will be compatible with the AIM-120 medium-range AAM. It will also embody extensive cockpit redesign. The final nine FRS Mk 1s were under construction at the beginning of 1988.

BRITISH AEROSPACE SEA HARRIER FRS MK 2

Dimensions: Span, 27 ft 3 in (8,31 m); length, 46 ft 3 in (14,10 m); height, 12 ft 2 in (3,71 m).

BROMON BR-2000

Country of Origin: USA.
Type: Light utility transport.
Power Plant: Two 1,870 shp General Electric CT7-9B turbo-props.
Performance: (Estimated) Max cruise speed, 258 mph (415 km/h); normal cruise, 242 mph (389 km/h); max initial climb, 1,790 ft/min (9,1 m/sec); service ceiling, 25,000 ft (7 620 m); range (with 9,000-lb/4 082-kg payload), 1,150 mls (1 850 km), (with max fuel and 5,855-lb/2 656-kg payload), 2,418 mls (3 890 km); ferry range, 2,650 mls (4 265 km).
Weights: Empty, 14,545 lb (6 600 kg); max take-off, 29,750 lb (13 495 kg).
Accommodation: Flight crew of two and up to 46 passengers four abreast with central aisle, or (military transport), max of 50 personnel, 35 combat-equipped troops or three 463L standard military pallets.
Status: First of three prototypes scheduled to enter flight test late 1988, with certification and commencement of initial deliveries in March 1989. Planned production rate of two aircraft monthly.
Notes: A non-pressurised aircraft of fundamentally simple design and largely conventional metal construction, the BR-2000 has been designed specifically for rough-field operation with minimal maintenance facilities in the undeveloped areas of the world. Intended as a multi-mission aircraft for both civil and military use, its envisaged roles include border patrol, forestry surveillance and medevac, up to 36 stretcher patients being accommodated for the last-mentioned mission, and provision is being made for three hardpoints on each wing for external stores. A quick-change interior will enable the BR-2000 to be adapted rapidly for combined passenger/cargo or all-cargo configurations.

BROMON BR-2000

Dimensions: Span, 82 ft 4 in (25,09 m); length, 77 ft 1 in (23,49 m); height, 27 ft 8 in (8,43 m).

CANADAIR CL-215T

Country of Origin: Canada.

Type: Multi-purpose amphibian.

Power Plant: Two 2,380 shp Pratt & Whitney PW123AF turboprops.

Performance: (Estimated) Max cruising speed, 221 mph (356 km/h) at 5,000 ft (1 525 m); max initial climb, 1,220 ft/min (6,2 m/sec); ferry range (with 1,950-lb/884-kg payload), 1,294 mls (2 082 km).

Weights: Operational empty (fire-fighting configuration), 26,400 lb (11 975 kg); max take-off (utility), 37,700 lb (17 100 kg), (fire-fighting), 43,850 lb (19 890 kg).

Accommodation: Flight crew of two (fire-fighting) and up to 26 passengers in transport configuration. Max payload of 10,560 lb (4 790 kg) in utility version and max disposable payload (fire-fighting) of 13,500 lb (6 123 kg).

Status: First of two CL-215T prototypes (produced from modifying existing CL-215 airframes) scheduled to fly in December 1988, with certification following in November 1989, and production aircraft available from the first quarter of 1990.

Notes: The CL-215T is a modernised, turboprop-powered version of the piston-engined CL-215 (see 1987 edition) of which 100 had been delivered by the beginning of 1988, with 11 remaining to be delivered at a rate of one monthly. The CL-215T will succeed the CL-215 in production, but the latter can be modified to the new standard, which, apart from the new engines, includes introduction of cockpit air conditioning and pressure refuelling. New production aircraft will also have a four-door, four-tank water drop system, increased water capacity and powered controls.

CANADAIR CL-215T

Dimensions: Span, 93 ft 10 in (28,60 m); length, 65 ft $0\frac{1}{4}$ in (19,82 m); height (on land), 29 ft $5\frac{1}{2}$ in (8,98 m); wing area, 1,080 sq ft (100,33 m²).

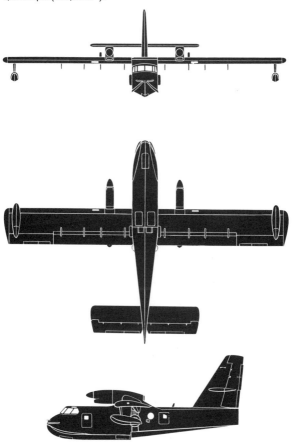

CANADAIR CHALLENGER 601-3A

Country of Origin: Canada.
Type: Light corporate transport.
Power Plant: Two 9,140 lb st (4 146 kgp) General Electric CF34-3A turbofans.
Performance: Max cruise speed, 529 mph (815 km/h), or Mach = 0·8; normal cruise, 509 mph (819 km/h), or Mach = 0·77; range cruise, 488 mph (786 km/h), or Mach = 0·74; operational ceiling, 41,000 ft (12 500 m); range (five passengers and IFR reserves), 3,947 mls (6 352 km), (long-range option from 1989), 4,145 mls (6 671 km).
Weights: Manufacturer's empty, 24,685 lb (11 197 kg); max take-off, 43,100 lb (19 550 kg). Long-range option from 1989: empty, 24,885 lb (11 288 kg); max take-off, 44,600 lb (20 230 kg).
Accommodation: Flight crew of two with customer-specified main cabin arrangements for up to 19 passengers.
Status: Prototype Challenger 601 flown on 10 April 1982, and first 601-3A flown on 28 September 1986, with 17 of latter delivered by beginning of 1988 when 163 Challengers (all versions) delivered and production continuing at 1·5 monthly.
Notes: The Challenger 601-3A is the latest version of the Model 601 which is the intercontinental-range derivative of the transcontinental Challenger 600. Development of a regional airliner derivative had been initiated by the beginning of 1988, this being intended to fly 1,000 mls (1 610 km) at 488 mph (785 km/h) with 48 passengers, or 1,400 mls (2 253 km) with 10,000 lb (4 536 kg) of freight. Embodying an 18 ft 9 in (5,71 m) stretch, this version will have four-abreast seating at 32-in (81-cm) pitch. From the first quarter of 1989, the Model 601-3A will be available with increased tankage (see above).

CANADAIR CHALLENGER 601-3A

Dimensions: Span, 64 ft 4 in (19,61 m); length, 68 ft 5 in (20,85 m); height, 20 ft 8 in (6,30 m); wing area, 450 sq ft (41,82 m²).

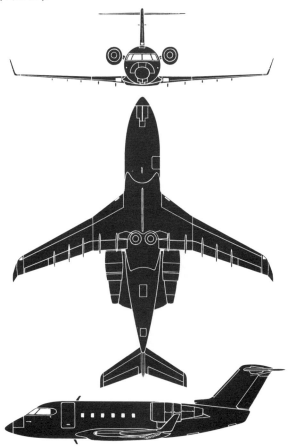

CASA C-101DD AVIOJET

Country of Origin: Spain.

Type: Tandem two-seat basic/advanced trainer and light tactical support aircraft.

Power Plant: One 4,700 lb st (2 130 kg) Garrett TFE731-5-1J turbofan.

Performance: Max speed, 519 mph (834 km/h) at 15,000 ft (4 570 m), 500 mph (805 km/h) at sea level; max initial climb, 6,100 ft/min (30,99 m/sec); time to 25,000 ft (7 620 m), 6·5 min; tactical radius (interdiction with cannon and four 551-lb/250-kg bombs, and 7% reserves), 322 mls (519 km) LO-LO-LO; ferry range (30 min reserves), 2,303 mls (3 706 km).

Weights: Loaded (training mission), 10,075 lb (4 570 kg); max take-off, 13,889 lb (6 300 kg).

Armament: One 30-mm cannon in ventral pod and up to 4,000 lb (1 815 kg) of ordnance on six wing stations.

Status: The C-101DD commenced flight testing on 20 May 1985. First C-101 flown on 29 June 1977, and 88 (C-101EB) delivered to Spanish Air Force, four (C-101BB) to Honduras and 16 (C-101CC) were in process of delivery to Jordan at the beginning of 1988. In addition, Chile is purchasing 37 (17 C-101BB and 20 C-101CC) of which all but first five are being assembled by ENAER.

Notes: The C-101DD is an enhanced version of the dual-role C-101CC (illustrated above) with a similar uprated engine, but additional avionics including a head-up display, weapon aiming computer, inertial attitude and heading reference system, and Doppler velocity sensor. The ENAER-assembled C-101CC is known as the A-36 Halcón (Hawk) and is equipped to carry the BAeD Sea Eagle anti-shipping missile. A reconnaissance pack and laser target designator are optional for both the C-101CC and DD versions. No orders had been announced for the C-101DD by the beginning of 1988.

CASA C-101DD AVIOJET

Dimensions: Span, 34 ft 9⅜ in (10,60 m); length, 41 ft 0 in (12,50 m); height, 13 ft 11 in (4,25 m); wing area, 215·3 sq ft (20,00 m²).

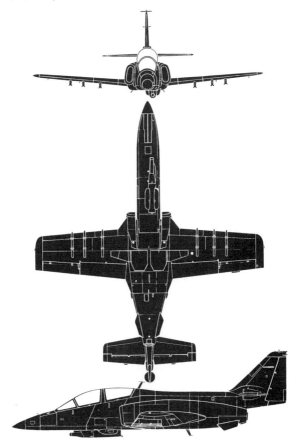

CASA-IPTN CN-235-100

Countries of Origin: Spain and Indonesia.

Type: Regional commercial transport and (CN-235M) military freighter.

Power Plant: Two 1,750 shp General Electric CT7-9C turbo-props.

Performance: Max cruise speed, 281 mph (452 km/h) at 15,000 ft (4 570 m); max initial climb, 1,525 ft/min (7,75 m/sec); range (max payload and reserves), 239 mls (385 km); ferry range, 2,429 mls (3 910 km).

Weights: Operational empty (typical), 20,725 lb (9 400 kg); max take-off, 31,745 lb (14 400 kg).

Accommodation: Flight crew of two and (regional airliner) seating arrangements for 39–44 passengers, (combi) 18 passengers and two LD-3 containers, or (freighter) four LD-3 containers or two 88 by 125 in (2,23 by 3,17 m) pallets.

Status: First prototype flown (in Spain) on 11 November 1983, and second (in Indonesia) on 31 December 1983. First production aircraft flown (in Spain) on 19 August 1986, and first customer delivery (Merpati-Nusantara) in following December. Total of 115 (both military and civil versions) on order by beginning of 1988 when production rate was rising to two monthly (one each from the Spanish and Indonesian assembly lines).

Notes: Initial version of CN-235 with CT7-7A engines being supplanted from third quarter of 1988 by CN-235-100. The CN-235 is produced jointly by CASA in Spain and IPTN in Indonesia on a 50–50 basis without component duplication. The military CN-235M has been ordered by Botswana, Panama and Saudi Arabia, and a maritime surveillance and ASW version has been ordered by the Indonesian Navy. Stretched version for 60–70 passengers, the CN-260, under study at the beginning of 1988.

CASA-IPTN CN-235-100

Dimensions: Span, 84 ft 7¾ in (25,81 m); length, 70 ft 0½ in (21,35 m); height, 26 ft 9¾ in (8,17 m); wing area, 636·17 sq ft (59,10 m²).

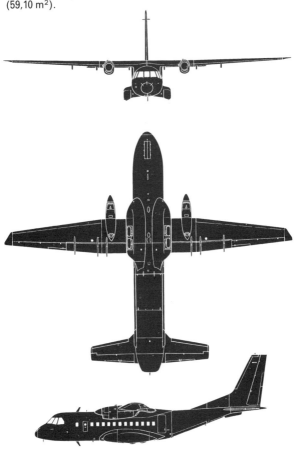

CESSNA 208 CARAVAN I

Country of Origin: USA.
Type: Light utility transport.
Power Plant: One 600 shp Pratt & Whitney Canada PT6A-114 turboprop.
Performance: Max cruise speed, 212 mph (341 km/h) at 10,000 ft (3 050 m), 203 mph (326 km/h) at 20,000 ft (6 095 m); initial climb, 1,050 ft/min (5,33 m/sec); service ceiling, 25,500 ft (7 775 m); range, 1,490 mls (2 398 km) at max range power at 20,000 ft (6 095 m) with 45 min reserves.
Weights: Standard empty, 3,862 lb (1 752 kg); max take-off, 8,000 lb (3 629 kg).
Accommodation: Pilot and (limited by FAR Pt 23) nine passengers, with optional arrangements (with FAR Pt 23 waiver) for 10 and 14 passengers with utility seating. Max useful load of 4,173 lb (1 893 kg).
Status: Engineering prototype flown 9 December 1982, and customer deliveries (to Federal Express) of Model 208A commencing February 1985. The stretched Model 208B (illustrated opposite) flown on 3 March 1986, with deliveries commencing following month. Approximately 190 (both versions) delivered by beginning of 1988.
Notes: The data above relate to the Model 208A, the Model 208B (illustrated by the general arrangement drawing) being a variant with a lengthened fuselage. A military derivative, the U-27A, can be fitted with an external reconnaissance pod with wide-angle camera and infra-red scanner. It is capable of loitering on station at 104 mph (167 km/h) at 5,000 ft (1 525 m) for 6·5 hours.

Dimensions: (208A): Span, 51 ft 8 in (15,75 m); length, 37 ft 7 in (11,46 m); height, 14 ft 10 in (4,52 m); wing area, 279·4 sq ft (25,96 m²).

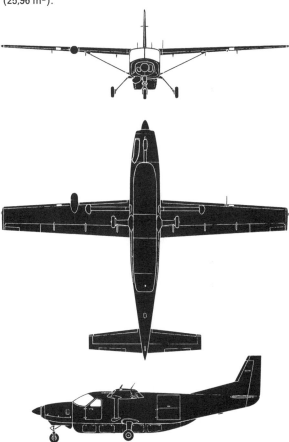

CESSNA CITATION 5

Country of Origin: USA.
Type: Light corporate executive transport.
Power Plant: Two 2,900 lb st (1 315 kgp) Pratt & Whitney JT15D-5A turbofans.
Performance: Max cruise (at 13,000 lb/5 897 kg), 492 mph (791 km/h) at 33,000 ft (10 060 m); max initial climb, 3,650 ft/min (18,54 m/sec); time to 41,000 ft (12 495 m), 24 min; max ceiling, 45,000 ft (13 715 m); range (at econ cruise with 45 min reserves and six passengers), 2,210 mls (3 558 km).
Weights: Max zero-fuel, 11,200 lb (5 080 kg); max take-off, 15,900 lb (7 212 kg).
Accommodation: Flight crew of two and standard seating for eight passengers.
Status: First prototype Citation 5 flown on 18 August 1987, and a pre-series prototype was scheduled to fly in January 1988, with initial deliveries planned for early 1989 and 35 to be manufactured during first year of production.
Notes: The Citation 5 has been developed to replace the Citation S/II (see 1984 edition). It differs from its predecessor primarily in having 16 per cent more power, a 20-in (51-cm) fuselage stretch and 25 per cent more horizontal tail surface area. The earlier Citation S/II serves with the US Navy as the T-47A for training personnel in the use of radar equipment. The T-47A differs from the S/II in having JT15D-5 turbofans in place of the 2,500 lb st (1 134 kgp) JT15D-4B engines and a reduced wing span to increase climb and permit $M = 0.733$ at 40,000 ft (12 190 m).

CESSNA CITATION 5

Dimensions: Span, 51 ft 8½ in (15,76 m); length, 48 ft 8½ in (14,84 m); height, 15 ft 0 in (4,57 m); wing area, 322·9 sq ft (30,00 m²).

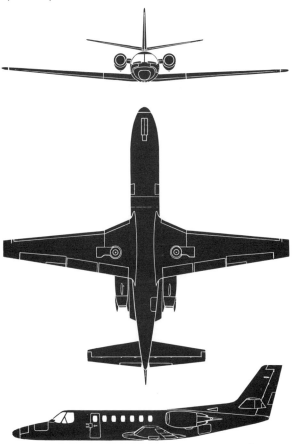

CLAUDIUS DORNIER SEASTAR

Country of Origin: Federal Germany.
Type: Light utility amphibian.
Power Plant: Two 500 shp Pratt & Whitney Canada PT6A-112 turboprops.
Performance: (At 8,810 lb/4 000 kg) Max cruise speed, 212 mph (341 km/h) at 10,000 ft (3 050 m); initial climb, 1,800 ft/min (8,0 m/sec); service ceiling, 28,000 ft (8 600 m); range (12 passengers and 10 per cent reserves), 345 mls (555 km), (with 1,000-lb/450-kg payload), 957 mls (1 540 km); ferry range, 1,150 mls (1 850 km).
Weights: Standard empty, 5,291 lb (2 400 kg); max take-off, 9,259 lb (4 200 kg).
Accommodation: Flight crew of two and maximum of 12 passengers in main cabin, or (medevac mission) five stretcher cases and two medical attendants.
Status: Prototype flown on 17 August 1984, and first pre-series aircraft flown on 24 April 1987, with second scheduled to join test programme spring 1988. Delivery of first series aircraft planned for mid 1989. Twenty-three options had been taken on the Seastar by the beginning of 1988.
Notes: Under development by Claudius Dornier Seastar GmbH, the Seastar is of all-composite construction and is intended for a wide range of roles including maritime surveillance, search and rescue, air ambulance and corporate transportation. The hull is primarily of glassfibre and graphite/epoxy which offer high corrosion resistance, and the Seastar is suitable for operation from grass, water, ice and snow surfaces.

CLAUDIUS DORNIER SEASTAR

Dimensions: Span, 50 ft 10¼ in (15,50 m); length, 40 ft 10½ in (12,46 m); height (on wheels), 15 ft 1 in (4,60 m); wing area, 306·55 sq ft (28,48 m²).

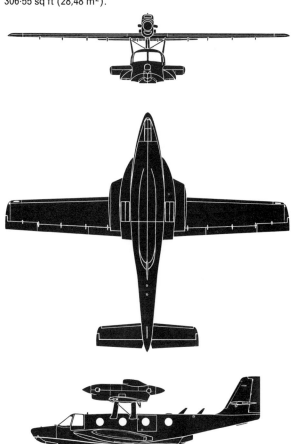

CNAMC A-5M(FANTAN)

Country of Origin: China.
Type: Single-seat close air support and ground attack aircraft.
Power Plant: Two 6,614 lb st (3 000 kgp) dry and 8,267 lb st (3 750 kgp) reheat Shenyang WP-6A turbojets.
Performance: Max speed, 761 mph (1 225 km/h), or Mach = 1·2, at 35,000 ft (10 975 m); combat radius (with 4,410 lb/ 2 000 kg external stores), 248 mls (400 km) LO-LO-LO, 373 mls (600 km) HI-LO-HI; max range (with max external fuel), 1,243 mls (2 000 km); ceiling, 52,495 ft (16 000 m).
Weights: Empty, 14,625 lb (6 634 kg); max take-off, 26,455 lb (12 000 kg).
Armament: Two 23-mm Type 2H cannon plus up to 4,410 lb (2 000 kg) of ordnance distributed between two fuselage and six wing stations.
Status: The A-5M is scheduled to enter test late 1988, with initial deliveries following during 1989 in succession to current A-5 III (A-5C). A-5 first flown 5 June 1965 and since manufactured in progressively upgraded versions.
Notes: The A-5M (illustrated on opposite page) is fundamentally similar to the A-5 III (illustrated above) apart from having marginally more powerful engines and effectively the avionics of the Italo-Brazilian AMX (ranging radar, head-up display, dual central computers, an air data computer and an inertial navigator). Manufactured by CNAMC (China Nanchang Aircraft Manufacturing Co) and HAC (Hongdu Aircraft Corporation), the A-5 has been derived from the Soviet MiG-19SF, and has been exported to Pakistan and North Korea.

CNAMC A-5M (FANTAN)

Dimensions: Span, 31 ft 10 in (9,70 m); length (excluding probe), 50 ft $6\frac{7}{8}$ in (15,41 m); height, 14 ft $9\frac{1}{2}$ in (4,51 m); wing area, 300·85 sq ft (27,95 m^2).

DASSAULT-BREGUET ATLANTIQUE G2 (ATL2)

Country of Origin: France.

Type: Long-range maritime patrol aircraft.

Power Plant: Two 5,665 shp Rolls-Royce/SNECMA Tyne RTy 20 Mk 21 turboprops.

Performance: Max speed, 368 mph (593 km/h) at sea level; normal cruise, 345 mph (556 km/h) at 25,000 ft (7 620 m); typical patrol speed, 196 mph (315 km/h); initial climb, 2,000 ft/min (10,1 m/sec); service ceiling, 30,000 ft (9 100 m); typical mission, 8 hrs patrol at 690 mls (1 110 km) from base at 2,000–3,000 ft (610–915 m); max range, 5,590 mls (9 000 km).

Weights: Empty equipped, 56,658 lb (25 700 kg); normal loaded weight, 97,442 lb (44 200 kg); max take-off, 101,850 lb (46 200 kg).

Accommodation: Normal flight crew of 12, comprising two pilots, flight engineer, forward observer, radio navigator, ESM/ECM/MAD operator, radar operator, tactical co-ordinator, two acoustic operators and two aft observers.

Armament: Up to eight Mk 46 homing torpedoes, nine 550-lb (250-kg) bombs or 12 depth charges, plus two AM 39 Exocet ASMs in forward weapons bay. Four wing stations with combined capacity of 6,614 lb (3 000 kg).

Status: First of two prototypes (converted from ATL1s) flown 8 May 1981, and production authorised on 24 May 1984 with initial batch of 16 aircraft. Deliveries between 1989 and 1996 to fulfil an *Aéronavale* requirement for 30–35 aircraft.

Notes: The Atlantique G2 (*Génération* 2) is a modernised version of the Atlantic G1, production of which terminated in 1973 after completion of 87 series aircraft.

DASSAULT-BREGUET ATLANTIQUE G2 (ATL2)

Dimensions: Span, 122 ft 7 in (37,36 m); length, 107 ft 0¼ in (32,62 m); height, 37 ft 1¼ in (11,31 m); wing area, 1,295·3 sq ft (120,34 m²).

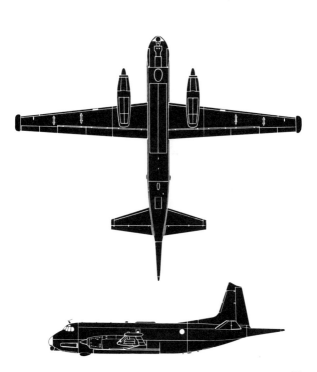

DASSAULT-BREGUET MIRAGE 2000

Country of Origin: France.
Type: Single-seat (2000DA) air superiority (2000N) two-seat low-altitude attack fighter or (2000B) conversion trainer.
Power Plant: One 14,460 lb st (6 500 kgp) dry and 21,385 lb st (9 700 kgp) reheat SNECMA M53-P2 turbofan.
Performance: Max speed (short endurance dash), 1,550 mph (2 495 km/h) above 36,090 ft (11 000 m), or Mach = 2·35, (continuous), 1,452 mph (2 337 km/h), or Mach = 2·2, (low-altitude without reheat and with eight 551-lb/250-kg bombs), 695 mph (1 118 km/h), or Mach = 0·912; max initial climb, 56,000 ft/min (284,5 m/sec); combat radius (intercept mission with two 374 Imp gal/1 700 l drop tanks and four AAMs), 435 mls (700 km).
Weights: (2000DA) Empty, 16,534 lb (7 500 kg); max take-off, 37,480 lb (17 000 kg).
Armament: Two 30-mm DEFA 554 cannon and (air superiority) two Matra 550 Magic and two Matra Super 530D AAMs, or (close support) up to 13,890 lb (6 300 kg) of ordnance on five fuselage and four wing stations.
Status: First of seven prototypes flown 10 March 1978, with production tempo of six monthly at beginning of 1988 when orders comprised 225 (129 2000DAs, 21 2000Bs and 75 2000Ns) for France, 36 for Abu Dhabi, 20 for Egypt, 40 for Greece, 49 for India and 12 for Peru.
Notes: The Mirage 2000 is currently being manufactured in four versions: the 2000DA optimised for the air superiority role, the 2000B two-seat trainer, the 2000R single-seat recce aircraft (for Abu Dhabi) and the 2000N low-altitude two-seat penetration aircraft (see 1985 edition). The last-mentioned is to enter *Armée de l'Air* service in July 1988 with terrain-following and ground-mapping radar.

DASSAULT-BREGUET MIRAGE 2000

Dimensions: Span, 29 ft 11½ in (9,13 m); length, 47 ft 1¼ in (14,36 m); height, 17 ft 0¾ in (5,20 m); wing area, 441·3 sq ft (41,000 m²).

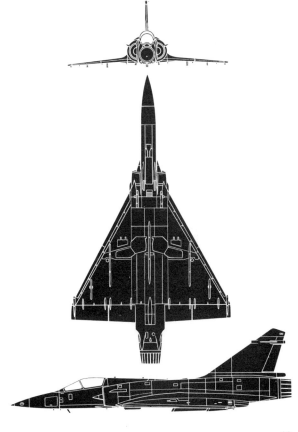

DASSAULT-BREGUET
MYSTERE-FALCON 900

Country of Origin: France.

Type: Light corporate transport.

Power Plant: Three 4,500 lb st (2 040 kgp) Garrett TFE 731-5A-1C turbofans.

Performance: Max speed, 574 mph (924 km/h) at 36,000 ft (10 975 m), or Mach = 0·87; max cruise, 554 mph (892 km/h) at 39,000 ft (11 890 m), or Mach = 0·84; long-range cruise, 495 mph (797 km/h) at 37,000 ft (11 275 m), or Mach = 0·75; max fuel range (IFR reserves), 4,486 mls (7 220 km); max payload range, 3,915 mls (6 300 km).

Weights: Operational empty (typical) 22,420 lb (10 170 kg); max take-off, 45,500 lb (20 640 kg).

Accommodation: Flight crew of two and optional main cabin arrangements for 8–15 passengers, with maximum seating for 19 passengers.

Status: Two prototypes flown on 21 September 1984 and 30 August 1985, with first production aircraft following in March 1986, and first customer deliveries commencing 19 December 1986. Production tempo scheduled attained four aircraft monthly by September 1987, with 25 delivered before end of the year. Sales exceeded 50 by the beginning of 1988, when production was continuing at four monthly.

Notes: The Mystère-Falcon 900 has been derived from the Falcon 50 (see 1982 edition) with which it shares some limited component commonality, being scaled up approximately 10 per cent by comparison with the earlier aircraft and having more powerful engines.

DASSAULT-BREGUET MYSTERE-FALCON 900

Dimensions: Span, 63 ft 5 in (19,33 m); length, 66 ft 3⅔ in (20,21 m); height, 24 ft 9¼ in (7,55 m); wing area, 527·77 sq ft (49,03 m²).

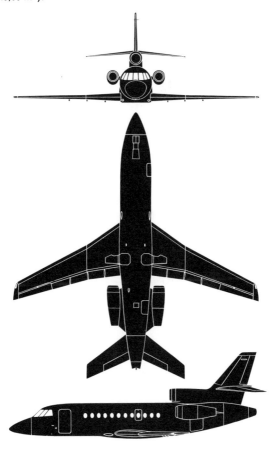

DASSAULT-BREGUET RAFALE A

Country of Origin: France.
Type: Single-seat advanced fighter technology demonstrator.
Power Plant: Two 16,000 lb st (7 258 kgp) reheat General Electric F404-GE-100 turbofans.
Performance: Max design speed, 1,320 mph (2 124 km/h) above 36,000 ft (10 975 m), or Mach = 2·0, 920 mph (1 480 km/h) at sea level, or Mach = 1·2.
Weights: Empty, 20,950 lb (9 500 kg); loaded (with two Magic and four Mica AAMs), 30,864 lb (14 000 kg); max take-off, 44,090 lb (20 000 kg).
Armament: Provision for one 30-mm DEFA 554 cannon and 12 external stores stations. Typical air defence armament comprises four medium-range Mica and two short-range Magic 2 AAMs.
Status: Single Rafale A prototype flown on 4 July 1986.
Notes: The Rafale (Squall) A is intended to demonstrate the technology (digital fly-by-wire control, relaxed stability, electronic cockpit and structural use of composites and aluminium-lithium) to be used in the Rafale D intended to fulfil both *Armée de l'Air* and *Aéronavale* (Rafale M) multi-role fighter requirements in the mid 'nineties. To be powered by two 16,535 lb st (7 500 kgp) reheat SNECMA M 88-15 engines, the Rafale D will be both smaller and lighter than the demonstration aircraft, with an equipped empty weight of 18,740 lb (8 500 kg) and a wing area of 473·63 sq ft (44,00 m²). Rafale D flight testing is expected to commence in October 1990, five prototypes being involved in the programme, one being a navalised aircraft (Rafale M) and one being a two-seater. Current planning calls for delivery of the first production Rafale D in July 1996.

DASSAULT-BREGUET RAFALE A

Dimensions: Span (with wingtip missiles), 36 ft 8⅛ in (11,18 m); length, 51 ft 10 in (15,79 m); height, 16 ft 11⅞ in (5,18 m); wing area, 506 sq ft (47,00 m²).

DASSAULT-BREGUET/DORNIER
ALPHA JET 2

Countries of Origin: France and Federal Germany.

Type: Tandem two-seat advanced trainer and light tactical support aircraft.

Power Plant: Two 3,175 lb st (1 440 kgp) SNECMA/Turboméca Larzac 04-C20 turbofans.

Performance: Max speed (clean), 572 mph (920 km/h) or Mach=0·86 at 32,800 ft (10 000 m); 645 mph (1 038 km/h) at sea level; max initial climb, 11,220 ft/min (57 m/sec); service ceiling, 48,000 ft (14 630 m); tactical radius (LO-LO-LO with gun pod, two 137·5 Imp gal/625 l drop tanks and underwing ordnance), 391 mls (630 km), (without drop tanks), 242 mls (390 km), (HI-LO-HI with drop tanks), 668 mls (1 075 km), (without drop tanks), 363 mls (583 km).

Weights: Empty equipped, 7,749 lb (3 515 kg); max take-off, 17,637 lb (8 000 kg).

Armament: (Tactical air support) Max of 5,510 lb (2 500 kg) of ordnance distributed between five stations.

Status: The Alpha Jet 2 entered flight test on 9 April 1982. Four delivered to Egypt in following year by parent company, and co-production with Egyptian industry continuing at rate of two per month at beginning of 1988 against Egyptian orders for 30 of (MS1) training and 30 of (MS2) attack versions. Six of MS2 version ordered by Cameroun.

Notes: The Alpha Jet 2 is an improved version of the basic aircraft with a new nav/attack system similar to that of the MS2 version, uprated engines and provision for Matra Magic AAMs. The proposed Alpha Jet 3, announced in June 1987, is an advanced training version with state-of-the-art cockpit controls and displays.

DASSAULT-BREGUET/DORNIER ALPHA JET 2

Dimensions: Span, 29 ft 11 in (9,11 m); length, 40 ft 3 in (12,29 m); height, 13 ft 9 in (4,19 m); wing area, 188 sq ft (17,50 m²).

DE HAVILLAND CANADA DASH 8-300

Country of Origin: Canada.
Type: Regional airliner.
Power Plant: Two 2,380 shp (flat-rated to 2,142 shp) Pratt & Whitney Canada PW123 turboprops.
Performance: Max cruise speed, 327 mph (526 km/h) at 15,000 ft (4 575 m), 322 mph (519 km/h) at 20,000 ft (6 095 m); max payload range, 575 mls (926 km); max range (long-range fuel capacity), 921 mls (1 482 km).
Weights: Operational empty (typical), 24,700 lb (11 204 kg), (with long-range tankage), 24,823 lb (11 260 kg); max take-off, 41,400 lb (18 643 kg).
Accommodation: Flight crew of two and standard arrangement for 50 passengers four abreast with central aisle, and optional arrangement for up to 56 passengers.
Status: Dash 8-300 prototype (converted from Dash 8-100) flown on 15 May 1987, and first two production -300s to join development programme May 1988, with first customer deliveries autumn 1988. Production of Dash 8 (all versions) scheduled to rise from three to four monthly by June 1988, increasing to five monthly by beginning of 1989. Approximately 90 Dash 8s delivered by beginning of 1988, when orders totalled 169 aircraft (plus 47 options).
Notes: The Dash 8-300 embodies an 11·25-ft (3,43-m) fuselage stretch, longer-span wing, strengthened undercarriage and more powerful engines. Proposed combi development with rear cargo door and movable bulkheads is designated -320C, other projected variants including the higher gross weight -320A and B, and the Dash 8-400 embodying further stretch and accommodating 70 passengers. This last-mentioned was under study at the beginning of 1988.

DE HAVILLAND CANADA DASH 8-300

Dimensions: Span, 90 ft 0 in (27,43 m); length, 84 ft 3 in (25,68 m); height, 24 ft 7 in (7,49 m); wing area, 605 sq ft (56,20 m²).

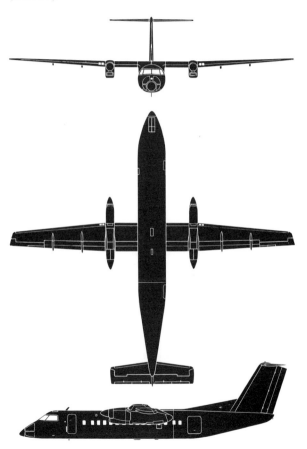

DORNIER DO 228

Country of Origin: Federal Germany.
Type: Light regional airliner and utility transport.
Power Plant: Two 715 shp Garrett AiResearch TPE 331-5-252D turboprops.
Performance: Max cruise speed, 268 mph (432 km/h) at 10,000 ft (3 280 m), 230 mph (370 km/h) at sea level; initial climb, 2,050 ft/min (10,4 m/sec); service ceiling, 29,600 ft (9 020 m); range (-100), 1,224 mls (1 970 km) at max range cruise, 1,075 mls (1 730 km) at max cruise, (-200), 715 mls (1 150 km) at max range cruise, 640 mls (1 030 km) at max cruise.
Weights: Operational empty (-100), 7,132 lb (3 235 kg), (-200), 7,450 lb (3 379 kg); max take-off, 12,570 lb (5 700 kg).
Accommodation: Flight crew of two and standard arrangements for (-100) 15 and (-200) 19 passengers in individual seats with central aisle.
Status: Prototype Do 228-100 flown on 28 March and -200 on 9 May 1981, and first customer delivery (A/S Norving) August 1982. A total of some 130 Do 228s (both -100s and -200s but excluding Indian production) had been ordered by beginning of December 1987, in which year production was four monthly.
Notes: The Do 228 mates a new-technology wing of super-critical section with the fuselage cross-section of the Do 128 (see 1982 edition), and two basic versions differing essentially in fuselage length and range capability are currently in production, the shorter-fuselage Do 228-100 and the longer-fuselage Do 228-200 (illustrated). All-cargo and corporate transport versions of the -100 are being offered. The -101, -201 and -202 versions offer progressively increased take-off weights. The -203F is a dedicated freighter. The Do 228 has been selected by India to meet that country's LTS (Light Transport Aircraft) requirement. Ten have been supplied by Dornier with 140 to be built in India by HAL.

DORNIER DO 228

Dimensions: Span, 55 ft 7 in (16,97 m); length, (-100) 49 ft 3 in (15,03 m), (-200), 54 ft 3 in (16,55 m); height, 15 ft 9 in (4,86 m); wing area, 344·46 sq ft (32,00 m²).

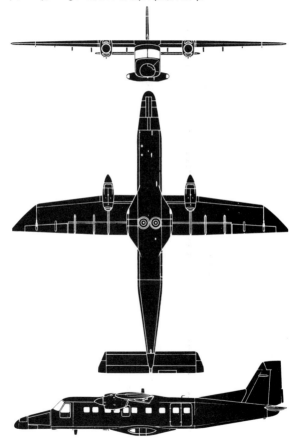

EMBRAER EMB-120 BRASILIA

Country of Origin: Brazil.

Type: Short-haul regional and corporate transport.

Power Plant: Two 1,800 shp Pratt & Whitney Canada PW118 turboprops.

Performance: Max cruise speed, 345 mph (556 km/h) at 22,000 ft (6 705 m); long-range cruise, 299 mph (482 km/h) at 25,000 ft (7 620 m); max initial climb, 2,120 ft/min (10,77 m/sec); range (30 passengers plus fuel for 115-ml/185-km diversion and 45-min hold), 1,087 mls (1 750 km) at 25,000 ft (7 620 m), (max fuel and similar reserves), 1,853 mls (2 982 km).

Weights: Typical empty equipped, 15,554 lb (7 070 kg); max take-off, 25,353 lb (11 500 kg).

Accommodation: Flight crew of two and standard arrangement for 30 passengers three abreast. Optional arrangements for 24 and 26 passengers.

Status: The first of three prototypes was flown on 27 July 1983, with first customer delivery (to Atlantic Southeast Airlines) following in August 1985. In August 1988 production tempo will be raised from four to five aircraft monthly. Orders totalled 128 aircraft (plus 129 options) by December 1987, 43 having been scheduled for delivery in that year with 50 following during 1988.

Notes: The Brazilian Air Force has purchased two Brasilias (with two on option), and has total requirement for 24 for personnel and freight transportation. Maritime surveillance and airborne early warning versions are currently proposed for early 'nineties service. The first corporate executive version of the Brasilia was delivered during 1986, in which year the proportion of composites (mainly Kevlar, glassfibre and carbonfibre) used in the structure of the aircraft was increased to some 10 per cent of the basic equipped empty weight.

EMBRAER EMB-120 BRASILIA

Dimensions: Span, 64 ft 10¾ in (19,78 m); length, 65 ft 7 in (20,00 m); height, 20 ft 10 in (6,35 m); wing area, 424·42 sq ft (39,43 m²).

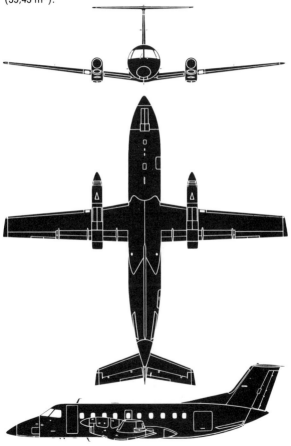

EMBRAER EMB-312 TUCANO

Country of Origin: Brazil.

Type: Tandem two-seat basic trainer.

Power Plant: One 750 shp Pratt & Whitney Canada PT6A-25C turboprop.

Performance: (At 5,622 lb/2 550 kg) Max speed, 269 mph (433 km/h) at 10,000 ft (3 050 m); max cruise, 255 mph (411 km/h); econ cruise, 198 mph (319 km/h); max initial climb, 2,180 ft/min (11,07 m/sec); max range (internal fuel with 30 min reserves), 1,145 mls (1 844 km); ferry range (two 145 Imp gal/660 l external tanks), 2,069 mls (3 330 km).

Weights: Basic empty, 3,991 lb (1 810 kg); max take-off (aerobatics), 5,622 lb (2 550 kg), (full weapon category), 7,000 lb (3 175 kg).

Armament: (Weapons training and light strike) Up to 2,205-lb (1 000 kg) of ordnance distributed between four wing stations.

Status: First of four prototypes flown on 15 August 1980, with deliveries to Brazilian Air Force (against order for 118) commencing September 1983 and completed May 1986. Twelve delivered to Honduras, 30 in process of delivery to Argentina, 20 delivered to Peru and 30 delivered to Venezuela. Assembly from kits being undertaken in Egypt against orders for 30 (plus options on 40) for the Egyptian Air Force and 80 (plus options on 20) for Iraqi Air Force after delivery by Embraer of 10 in fly-away condition. Licence manufacture of more powerful version for the RAF by Shorts (see pages 192–3).

Notes: Eighty used by Brazilian Academy for basic training, with remaining aircraft used for weapons training. Two Tucanos fitted with Garrett TPE331 engines by Embraer and flown on 14 February and 28 July 1986 respectively, the first being delivered to Shorts and the second being retained for development work.

EMBRAER EMB-312 TUCANO

Dimensions: Span, 36 ft $6\frac{1}{2}$ in (11,14 m); length, 32 ft $4\frac{1}{4}$ in (9,86 m); height, 11 ft $7\frac{7}{8}$ in (3,40 m); wing area, 208·82 sq ft (19,40 m²).

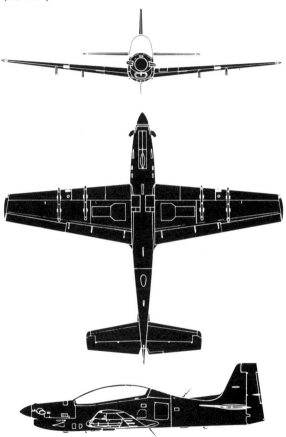

ENAER T-35 PILLAN

Country of Origin: Chile.

Type: Tandem two-seat primary/basic trainer.

Power Plant: One 300 hp Textron Lycoming AEIO-540-K1K5 six-cylinder horizontally-opposed engine.

Performance: (At max take-off weight) Max speed, 193 mph (311 km/h) at sea level; cruise (75% power), 185 mph (298 km/h) at 8,000 ft (2 680 m); max initial climb, 1,516 ft/min (7,7 m/sec); service ceiling, 19,100 ft (5 820 m); range (at 75% power with 45 min reserves), 679 mls (1 093 km).

Weights: Empty, 1,836 lb (832 kg); empty equipped, 2,048 lb (929 kg); max take-off, 2,900 lb (1 315 kg).

Armament: (Weapons training) Two pods of four or seven rockets, 250-lb (113,4-kg) bombs or 12,7-mm gun pods.

Status: First of two prototypes (assembled by Piper) flown 6 March 1981. Six pre-series aircraft assembled in Chile and first production aircraft flown 28 December 1984. Approx 50 delivered by beginning of 1988, when production rate was three monthly. Eighty ordered by Chilean Air Force and 40 (T-35C) by Spanish Air Force. Marketing commenced by Piper mid 1987.

Notes: The Pillán (Devil) was designed under contract by Piper and embodies some standard components of the PA-28, PA-31 and PA-32 series light aircraft. Manufacture has been progressively transferred to ENAER which is building two versions for the Chilean Air Force as the T-35A (60) and T-35C (40) with simple avionics kit for basic training and T-35B (20) with avionics for IFR instruction. A turboprop-powered derivative, the T-35TX Aucan (see 1987 edition) was flown on 14 February 1986, but development has been discontinued. The T-35C aircraft for the Spanish Air Force are assembled from kits by CASA as the Tamiz (Grader) the first of these having been flown on 12 May 1986.

Dimensions: Span, 28 ft 11 in (8,81 m); length, 26 ft 1 in (7,97 m); height, 7 ft 8⅛ in (2,34 m); wing area, 147 sq ft (13,64 m²).

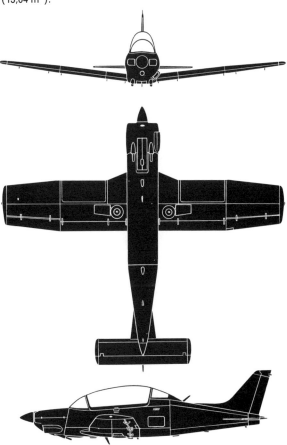

FAMA IA 63 PAMPA

Country of Origin: Argentina.
Type: Tandem two-seat basic/advanced trainer.
Power Plant: One 3,500 lb st (1 588 kgp) Garrett TFE371-2-2N turbofan.
Performance: Max speed, 509 mph (819 km/h) at 22,965 ft (7 000 m), 460 mph (740 km/h) at sea level; max cruise, 464 mph (747 km/h) at 13,125 ft (4 000 m); max initial climb, 5,315 ft/min (27 m/sec); service ceiling, 42,325 ft (12 900 m); range (clean), 930 mls (1 500 km) at 345 mph (560 km/h) at 13,125 ft (4 000 m); tactical radius (attack with 2,205 lb/1 000 kg external load), 224 mls (360 km) HI-LO-HI with 5 min over target and 30 min reserves.
Weights: Empty, 5,791 lb (2 627 kg); normal loaded, 8,377 lb (3 800 kg); max take-off, 11,022 lb (5 000 kg).
Armament: (Training or light attack) One 30-mm cannon pod on fuselage centreline and up to 2,557 lb (1 160 kg) ordnance distributed between four wing stations.
Status: Three prototypes flown on 6 October 1984, 7 August 1985 and 25 March 1986. First production Pampa was expected to fly in December 1987, with two more flying by April 1988, and total requirement of 64 aircraft. The Bolivian Air Force announced a requirement for 12 aircraft during 1987.
Notes: The Pampa has been developed by Dornier of Federal Germany which continues to provide assistance to the Fabrica Argentina de Material Aeroespacial (FAMA). The third prototype differs from its predecessors in having armament provisions and Stencel rather than Martin-Baker ejection seats. A version powered by a 4,300 lb st (1 950 kgp TFE731-5) is proposed as the standard series model and a shipboard version has been under consideration.

FAMA IA 63 PAMPA

Dimensions: Span, 31 ft 9½ in (9,69 m); length, 35 ft 10¼ in (10,93 m); height, 14 ft 0¾ in (4,29 m); wing area, 168·24 sq ft (15,63 m²).

FOKKER 50

Country of Origin: Netherlands.
Type: Regional airliner.
Power Plant: Two 2,250 shp Pratt & Whitney (Canada) PW125B turboprops.
Performance: Max cruise speed, 320 mph (515 km/h) at 21,000 ft (6 400 m); long-range cruise, 282 mph (454 km/h) at 25,000 ft (7 620 m); range with 50 passengers (at 41,865 lb/18 990 kg), 698 mls (1 124 km), (at 45,900 lb/20 820 kg), 1,826 mls (2 938 km).
Weights: Operational empty (typical), 27,850 lb (12 633 kg); max take-off (standard), 41,865 lb (18 990 kg), (optional), 45,900 lb (20 820 kg).
Accommodation: Flight crew of two and standard arrangement for 50 passengers four abreast, with optional high-density arrangement for 58–60 passengers or 46 business class passengers.
Status: First of two prototypes flown on 28 December 1985, with first production aircraft following on 13 February 1987 and first customer delivery (DLT) on 7 August 1987. Total of 52 aircraft on firm order and 14 on option by beginning of January 1988.
Notes: Based on the F27-500 Friendship (see 1982 edition), the Fokker 50 makes extensive use of composites in its structure and new-technology engines have been adopted, these driving six-bladed propellers.

Dimensions: Span, 95 ft $1\frac{3}{4}$ in (29,00 m); length, 83 ft $7\frac{3}{4}$ in (25,19 m); height, 28 ft $2\frac{1}{2}$ in (8,60 m); wing area, 753·5 sq ft (70,00 m²).

FOKKER 100

Country of Origin: Netherlands.
Type: Short/medium-haul commercial transport.
Power Plant: Two 13,320 lb st (6 042 kgp) Rolls-Royce RB183-03 Tay 620-15 turbofans.
Performance: Max cruise speed, 508 mph (817 km/h) at 37,000 ft (11 280 m), or Mach=0·77; econ cruise, 475 mph (765 km/h), or Mach=0·72; range (with 107 passengers), 1,678 mls (2 700 km) at econ cruise, (max fuel), 2,624 mls (4 223 km) at long-range cruise.
Weights: Typical operational empty, 53,695 lb (24 356 kg); max take-off, 95,000 lb (43 092 kg).
Accommodation: Flight crew of two and standard seating for 107 passengers five abreast with optional arrangements including 60 business class and 45 economy class passengers, or 12 first class and 80–85 economy class passengers.
Status: First of two prototypes flown on 30 November 1986, with Dutch certification obtained 20 November 1987, and first customer delivery (to Swissair) following in February 1988. Eighty-seven on firm order plus 91 on option at beginning of January 1988. Production building up to three monthly early in 1988.
Notes: Technically a derivative of the F28 Fellowship (see 1985 edition), the Fokker 100 makes extensive use of advanced technology, has new systems and equipment, a lengthened fuselage, aerodynamically redesigned and extended wings and new engines. Aircraft ordered by US Air will have max take-off weight increased to 98,000 lb (44 453 kg) and be powered by the 15,100 lb st (6 850 kgp) Tay 650-15 engine, but weights up to 105,000 lb (47 628 kg) are in prospect with the availability of the uprated Tay 660 engine.

FOKKER 100

Dimensions: Span, 92 ft 1½ in (28,08 m); length, 115 ft 10 in (35,31 m); height, 27 ft 10½ in (8,60 m); wing area, 977·4 sq ft (90,80 m²).

GAIGC FT-7 (JJ-7)

Country of Origin: China (USSR).

Type: Tandem two-seat combat-capable advanced conversion trainer.

Power Plant: One 9,700 lb st (4 400 kgp) dry and 13,448 lb st (6 100 kgp) reheat Chengdu WP-7B turbojet.

Performance: Max speed, 1,350 mph (2 175 km/h) or Mach = 2·05, above 36,090 ft (11 000 m); service ceiling, 56,760 ft (17 300 m); range (internal fuel), 628 mls (1 010 km), (with 158 Imp gal/720 l drop tank), 907 mls (1 459 km).

Weights: Empty, 11,750 lb (5 330 kg); normal loaded, 16,733 lb (7 590 kg); max take-off, 18,960 lb (8 600 kg).

Armament: (Weapon training and secondary operational role) One twin-barrel 23-mm GSh-23L cannon pod beneath fuselage centreline and wing stations for two PL-2B AAMs, two 18-round 57-mm rocket pods or two 551-lb (250 kg) bombs.

Status: First flown July 1985 as combat-capable two-seat derivative of F-7M single-seat fighter (see 1987 edition). Series production initiated 1987 for People's Republic of China Air Force (as JJ-7) by GAIGC (Guizhou Aviation Industry Group).

Notes: Closely resembling the Soviet MiG-21U, but possessing external contour differences, the FT-7 (export designation of the JJ-7) has a GEC-supplied avionics suite similar to that of the single-seat F-7M Airguard from which it is derived. The latter is the latest reverse-engineered derivative of the MiG-21F, and both FT-7 and F-7M are on offer to third world countries. Studies of upgraded versions with US engine (F404, PW1216 and PW1120) mated with lateral intakes have been undertaken. The FT-7 features a removable saddleback fuel tank aft of the rear cockpit and sideways-opening (to starboard) twin cockpit canopies.

GAIGC FT-7 (JJ-7)

Dimensions: Span, 23 ft 5⅝ in (7,15 m); length (excluding probe), 45 ft 9 in (13,94 m); height, 13 ft 5½ in (4,10 m); wing area, 247·6 sq ft (23,00 m²).

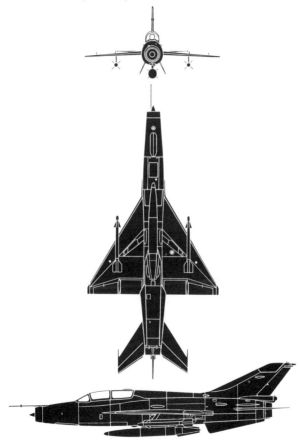

GATES LEARJET 31

Country of Origin: USA.

Type: Light corporate executive transport.

Power Plant: Two 3,500 lb st (1 588 kgp) Garrett TFE731-2-2B turbofans.

Performance: Max speed, 534 mph (860 km/h), or Mach = 0·78, at 25,000 ft (7 620 m); max cruise, 515 mph (828 km/h) at 41,000 ft (12 500 m); econ cruise, 460 mph (740 km/h) at 45,000 ft (13 700 m); max range (at econ cruise with 45 min reserves and four passengers), 1,877 mls (3 020 km) with standard fuel, 2,130 mls (3 428 km) with extended-range fuel.

Weights: Empty, 9,857 lb (4 471 kg); max take-off, 15,500 lb (7 030 kg).

Accommodation: Flight crew of two and up to a maximum of 10 passengers, with various optional cabin arrangements for four to eight passengers.

Status: First of two prototypes of the Model 31 flown in 1987, with certification scheduled for the second quarter of 1988 and initial customer deliveries following immediately afterwards.

Notes: The Model 31 mates the fuselage of the Model 35/36 to a modified wing of the very different Model 55 (which see) and employs similar delta fins on the lower rear fuselage to those adopted for the Model 55C, these eliminating the need for stall avoidance devices. Apart from wing and delta fins, the Model 31 is fundamentally similar to the Models 35 and 36 which differ one from the other in fuel capacity and accommodation. Eighty Model 35 Learjets serve with the USAF as C-21A operational support aircraft, and various special missions versions of the Models 35 and 36 are available, including the EC-35A (electronic warfare), PC-35A (maritime patrol) and RC-35A (reconnaissance).

GATES LEARJET 31

Dimensions: Span, 43 ft 9½ in (13,34 m); length, 48 ft 8 in (14,83 m); height, 12 ft 3 in (3,73 m); wing area, 264·5 sq ft (24,57 m).

GATES LEARJET 55C

Country of Origin: USA.

Type: Light corporate executive transport.

Power Plant: Two 3,700 lb st (1 678 kgp) Garrett TFE 731-3A-2B turbofans.

Performance: Max speed, 549 mph (884 km/h), or Mach = 0·81, at 30,000 ft (9 150 m); max cruise, 530 mph (853 km/h) at 41,000 ft (12 500 m); econ cruise, 486 mph (782 km/h) at 47,000 ft (14 325 m); max initial climb, 4,059 ft/min (20,62 m/sec); max ceiling, 51,000 ft (15 545 m); max range (at econ cruise with 45 min reserves and four passengers), 2,590 mls (4 170 km) with standard fuel, 2,925 mls (4 707 km) with long-range fuel.

Weights: Empty, 12,622 lb (5 725 kg); max take-off, 21,000 lb (9 526 kg).

Accommodation: Flight crew of two and standard seating for eight passengers with max of 10 passengers.

Status: Model 55C introduced September 1987 and scheduled for certification spring 1988. Latest series version of Model 55 of which first of two prototypes flown on 19 April 1979, with customer deliveries commencing April 1981.

Notes: The Model 55C differs from the preceding version, the Model 55B introduced in 1986 with fully-integrated all-digital cockpit, in having delta fins on the lower rear fuselage. These increase directional stability and improve pitch stability, affording better low-speed handling and allowing lower take-off, approach and landing speeds. In addition, the engine pylons are of new low-drag design. The Model 55C is available in basic form and with long-range tanks, and the basic model established both speed records and time-to-altitude records for its class in 1983.

GATES LEARJET 55C

Dimensions: Span, 43 ft 9½ in (13,34 m); length, 55 ft 1½ in (16,79 m); height, 14 ft 8 in (4,47 m); wing area, 264·5 sq ft (24,57 m).

GENERAL DYNAMICS F-16 FIGHTING FALCON

Country of Origin: USA.

Type: (F-16C) Single-seat multi-role fighter and (F-16D) two-seat operational trainer.

Power Plant: One 14,800 lb st (6 713 kgp) dry and 23,830 lb st (10 809 kgp) reheat Pratt & Whitney F100-PW-200 or -220, or 16,610 lb st (7 334 kgp) dry and 27,080 lb st (12 283 kgp) reheat General Electric F110-GE-100 turbofan.

Performance: (F-16C with F100-PW-200) Max speed (short endurance dash), 1,333 mph (2 145 km/h) at 40,000 ft (12 190 m) or Mach = 2·02, (sustained), 1,247 mph (2 007 km/h) or Mach = 1·89; tactical radius (HI-LO-HI interdiction on internal fuel), 360 mls (580 km) with six 500-lb (227-kg) bombs.

Weights: (F-16C) Take-off (intercept mission with AAMs), 25,070 lb (11 372 kg); max take-off, 37 500 lb (17 010 kg).

Armament: One 20-mm M61A-1 rotary cannon and (intercept) two to six AIM-9L/M AAMs, or (interdiction) up to 12,430 lb (5 638 kg) ordnance between nine stations.

Status: First of two (YF-16) prototypes flown 20 January 1974, and first production aircraft (F-16A) flown 7 August 1978, with first F-16C being delivered 19 July 1984. Total of 2,975 ordered by beginning of 1988 of which some 1,900 delivered and planned acquisition by 16 countries totalling 4,207. European multination programme embraces 160 for Belgium, 70 for Denmark, 72 for Norway and 213 for Netherlands. Other purchasers include Bahrain (12), Egypt (80), Greece (40), Indonesia (12), Israel (150), South Korea (36), Pakistan (40), Singapore (8), Thailand (12), Turkey (160) and Venezuela (24).

Notes: Upgraded F-16C and D have common engine bay for either F100 or F110 from 1986. The F-16C and F-16D aircraft ordered by Turkey are being licence-manufactured in that country with deliveries commencing in 1988. First Turkish-assembled F-16C flown on 11 October 1987, and production to peak at 1·5 monthly.

GENERAL DYNAMICS F-16 FIGHTING FALCON

Dimensions: Span (excluding missiles), 31 ft 0 in (9,45 m); length (excluding probe), 47 ft 7¾ in (14,52 m); height, 16 ft 8⅖ in (5,09 m); wing area, 300 sq ft (27,87 m²).

GRUMMAN A-6F INTRUDER II

Country of Origin: USA.

Type: Two-seat carrier-borne all-weather strike aircraft.

Power Plant: Two 10,800 lb st (4 900 kgp) General Electric F404-GE-400D turbofans.

Performance: (A-6E) Max speed, 644 mph (1 037 km/h) at sea level; optimum altitude cruise, 474 mph (763 km/h); max initial climb, 7,620 ft/min (38,71 m/sec); range (max military load), 1,011 mls (1 627 km), (max external fuel), 3,245 mls (5 222 km).

Weights: (A-6E) Empty, 26,746 lb (12 132 kg); max take-off (catapult), 58,600 lb (26 580 kg), (field), 60,400 lb (27,397 kg).

Armament: One fuselage centreline and six wing stores stations with max external ordnance load of 19,000 lb (8,618 kg).

Status: First of five planned development A-6F Intruder IIs flown 26 August 1987, with second following in November and third scheduled to join the flight test programme February 1988. US Navy planning late 1987 called for delivery of 150 between 1990 and 1995. However, the A-6F programme was being restructured early 1988, and was expected to include a mix of new-build A-6Fs and upgraded A-6Es.

Notes: The A-6F is a re-engined derivative of the Pratt & Whitney J52-P-8B-powered A-6E Intruder I with the new aluminium/composite wings to be fitted to the final 11 production A-6Es and retrofitted to earlier production aircraft and extensive equipment upgrading. Apart from enhanced radar embodying an air-air capability, the A-6F offers improved reliability and maintainability.

GRUMMAN A-6F INTRUDER II

Dimensions: Span, 53 ft 0 in (16,15 m); length, 54 ft 9 in (16,69 m); height, 16 ft 2 in (4,93 m); wing area, 528·9 sq ft (49,10 m²).

GRUMMAN E-2C HAWKEYE

Country of Origin: USA.

Type: Airborne early warning, surface surveillance and strike control aircraft.

Power Plant: Two 4,910 ehp Allison T56-A-425 or (from 1987) 5,250 ehp T56-A-427 turboprops.

Performance: (T56-A-425 engines and max take-off weight) Max speed, 372 mph (598 km/h); max cruise, 358 mph (576 km/h); initial climb, 2,515 ft/min (12,8 m/sec); service ceiling, 30,800 ft (9 390 m); time on station, 4 hrs at 200 mls (320 km) from base; ferry range, 1,604 mls (2 580 km).

Weights: Empty, 38,063 lb (17 265 kg); max take-off, 51,933 lb (23 556 kg).

Accommodation: Flight crew of two and Airborne Tactical Data System team of three.

Status: First of two E-2C prototypes flown 20 January 1971, with first production following 23 September 1972. Total of 113 ordered by US Navy, five by Egypt, four by Israel, eight by Japan and four by Singapore, with 120 built by beginning of 1988, when production planned to continue at six annually until at least 1995.

Notes: Evolved from the E-2A (56 built with 52 upgraded to E-2B standard), the E-2C differed fundamentally in replacing the 'blue water' capable APS-96 radar system with APS-120 capable of target detection and tracking over land. The improved APS-138 was retrofitted from 1983, and this is to give place to APS-139 in new production E-2Cs from 1988. The extended detection-range APS-145 less susceptible to overland clutter will be retrofitted to all aircraft from 1990. From 1987, uprated T56-A-427 engines were being installed and the central computer was being upgraded, with improved IFF and enhanced displays following during 1988.

GRUMMAN E-2C HAWKEYE

Dimensions: Span, 80 ft 7 in (24,56 m); length, 57 ft 7 in (17,55 m); height, 18 ft 4 in (5,69 m); wing area, 700 sq ft (65,03 m²).

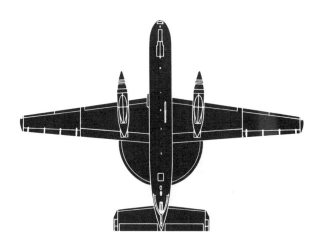

GRUMMAN F-14A (PLUS) TOMCAT

Country of Origin: USA.

Type: Two-seat shipboard multi-role fighter.

Power Plant: Two 16,610 lb st (7 334 kgp) dry and 27,080 lb st (12 283 kgp) reheat General Electric F110 GE-400 turbofans.

Performance: Max speed (with four semi-recessed AIM-7 missiles), 912 mph (1 468 km/h) at sea level, or Mach = 1·2, 1,544 mph (2 485 km/h) at 40,000 ft (12 190 m), or Mach = 2·34; combat air patrol loiter time (with two 267-US gal/1 011-l external tanks), 2·7 hrs; intercept radius (at Mach = 1·3), 510 mls (820 km).

Weights: (Estimated) Empty, 42,000 lb (19 050 kg); max take-off, 75,000 lb (34 020 kg).

Armament: One 20-mm M61A-1 rotary cannon and (typical) four AIM-54C Phoenix, two AIM-7 Sparrow and two AIM-9 Sidewinder air-to-air missiles.

Status: First of two F-14A (Plus) prototypes flown on 29 September 1986, and first of 38 new production F-14A (Plus) fighters accepted by US Navy in November 1987. Thirty-two existing F-14As to be remanufactured to similar standard before commencement of deliveries of definitive F-14D in 1990.

Notes: The F-14A (Plus) is an interim development of the F-14A pending availability of the F-14D which, with similar engines, will have upgraded avionics, including a new digital radar and much improved electronic countermeasures capability. F-14A (Plus) has combat air patrol time on station enhanced by 35 per cent.

GRUMMAN F-14A (PLUS) TOMCAT

Dimensions: Span (20 deg sweep), 64 ft 1½ in (19,55 m), (68 deg sweep), 37 ft 7 in (11,45 m); length, 61 ft 11⅞ in (18,90 m); height, 16 ft 0 in (4,88 m); wing area, 565 sq ft (52,50 m²).

GULFSTREAM AEROSPACE GULFSTREAM IV

Country of Origin: USA.
Type: Corporate transport.
Power Plant: Two 13,800 lb st (6 260 kgp) Rolls-Royce RB183-03 Tay Mk 610-8 turbofans.
Performance: Max cruise speed, 597 mph (962 km/h) at 36,000 ft (10 975 m), or Mach = 0·88; long-range cruise, 528 mph (850 km/h); or Mach = 0·8; initial climb, 3,816 ft/min (19,38 m/sec); max operating altitude, 51,000 ft (15 545 m); range (crew of three and eight passengers), 4,950 mls (7 968 km).
Weights: Manufacturer's empty, 35,200 lb (15 967 kg); max take-off, 71,700 lb (35 523 kg).
Accommodation: Flight crew of two or three, with standard optional arrangements for 12, 14 or 15 passengers.
Status: Prototype flown on 19 September 1985, with certification following on 22 April 1987, at which time initial customer deliveries commenced, with 44 having been scheduled for delivery by end of 1987, when approximately 130 had been ordered and 40 were due to be completed during 1988.
Notes: Essentially a progressive development of the Gulfstream III (see 1984 edition), the Gulfstream IV features a structurally redesigned wing, a lengthened fuselage and Tay engines in place of Speys. The new wing has 30 per cent fewer parts than the wing of the Gulfstream III. A military version, the Gulfstream SRA-4, was being offered at the beginning of 1988 for such missions as surveillance, reconnaissance, medical evacuation, administrative transport, priority freight, maritime patrol and ASW. Several derivative versions, including a stretched 24-seat airliner, were under consideration at the beginning of 1988. Twenty-four world speed records were claimed for a westbound round-the-world flight by the third production Gulfstream IV made 12–14 June 1987.

GULFSTREAM AEROSPACE GULFSTREAM IV

Dimensions: Span, 77 ft 10 in (23,72 m); length, 88 ft 4 in (26,90 m); height, 24 ft 10 in (7,60 m); wing area, 950·4 sq ft (88,30 m²).

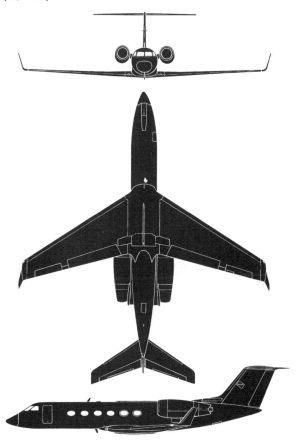

HARBIN SH-5

Country of Origin: China.
Type: Maritime patrol and surveillance, anti-submarine, search and rescue, and transport amphibian.
Power Plant: Four 3,150 ehp Shanghai WJ-5A-1 turboprops.
Performance: Max speed, 345 mph (555 km/h); max continuous cruise, 280 mph (456 km/h); minimum patrol speed (two engines), 143 mph (230 km/h); service ceiling, 22,965 ft (7 000 m); range (max fuel), 2,950 mls (4 750 km); max endurance (two engines), 12–15 hrs.
Weights: Empty equipped (ASW), 58,420 lb (26 500 kg), (SAR), 55,115 lb (25 000 kg); normal loaded, 79,365 lb (36 000 kg); max take-off, 99,206 lb (45 000 kg).
Accommodation: Flight crew of five (pilot, co-pilot, navigator, flight engineer and radio operator), plus systems/equipment operators according to mission.
Armament: Four underwing stores stations for two C-101 anti-shipping missiles (inboard) and two torpedoes (outboard).
Status: First of three prototypes flown on 3 April 1976, with service entry announced 3 September 1986. In service with two naval aviation units by beginning of 1988.
Notes: The SH-5 (Shui Hongzhaji – Maritime Bomber) has undergone a singularly leisurely development process. Also referred to by the westernised designation of PS-5 (indicating patrol seaplane) it is currently in service in maritime patrol and ASW form, and during the course of 1987, an ASW equipment and avionics upgrade was being sought, a fit based on that developed for the Dassault-Breguet Atlantique 2 being under consideration. Search and rescue, and transport versions of the SH-5 are reportedly under development by the Harbin Aircraft Manufacturing Corporation.

HARBIN SH-5

Dimensions: Span, 118 ft 1¼ in (36,00 m); length, 127 ft 7½ in (38,90 m); height, 32 ft 1½ in (9,79 m); wing area, 1,550 sq ft (144,00 m²).

HARBIN Y-12-2

Country of Origin: China.
Type: Light STOL general-purpose transport.
Power Plant: Two 620 shp Pratt & Whitney Canada PT6A-27 turboprops.
Performance: Max cruise speed, 204 mph (328 km/h) 9,840 ft (3 000 m); econ cruise, 143 mph (230 km/h) at 9,840 ft (3 000 m); max initial climb, 1,732 ft/min (8,8 m/sec); range (with max fuel and 1,762-lb/800-kg payload with 45 min reserves), 895 mls (1 440 km).
Weights: Empty, 6,256 lb (2 838 kg); operational, 7,608 lb (2 997 kg); max take-off, 11,684 lb (5 300 kg).
Accommodation: Flight crew of two with three-abreast seating in main cabin for up to 17 passengers. Alternative arrangements for aeromedical and all-cargo versions.
Status: The first of two prototypes (Y-12-1) flown on 14 July 1982, and first of three test and evaluation models of the series version (Y-12-2) flown in 1983. Chinese certification obtained in December 1985, and US certification expected during 1988. Production of 1·5–2·0 aircraft per month at beginning of 1988 when 24 had been completed.
Notes: Derived from the seven-seat piston-engined Y-11 (of which 40 were built) by the Harbin Aircraft Manufacturing Corporation, the Y-12-2 is a development of the Y-12-1 which differed essentially in having 500 shp PT6A-10 engines. A new cabin interior and environmental control system for the Y-12-2 have been developed by the Hong Kong Aircraft Engineering Company (HAECO), and drawings and kits have been supplied for application to aircraft on the Harbin assembly line.

HARBIN Y-12-2

Dimensions: Span, 456 ft 10½ in (17,23 m); length, 48 ft 9 in (14,86 m); height, 17 ft 3¾ in (5,27 m); wing area, 368·88 sq ft (34,27 m²).

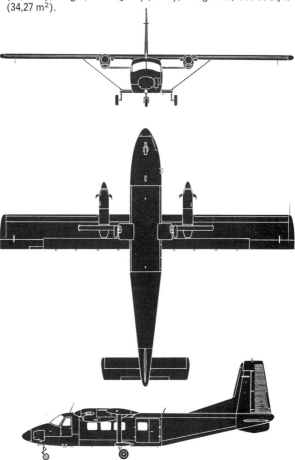

ILYUSHIN IL-76 (CANDID)

Country of Origin: USSR.

Type: Heavy-duty medium/long-haul military and commercial freighter and troop transport.

Power Plant: Four 26,455 lb st (12 000 kgp) Soloviev D-30KP turbofans.

Performance: Max speed, 528 mph (850 km/h) at 32,810 ft (10 000 m); max cruise, 497 mph (800 km/h) at 29,500–42,650 ft (9 000–13 000 m); range cruise, 466 mph (750 km/h); initial climb, 1,772 ft/min (9,0 m/sec); range (with max payload), 1,864 mls (3 000 km) with 45 min reserves, (with 44,032-lb/20 000-kg payload), 4,040 mls (6 500 km).

Weights: Max take-off, 374,790 lb (170 000 kg).

Armament: (Military) Twin 23-mm cannon in tail barbette.

Accommodation: Normal flight crew of seven (including two freight handlers) with navigator's compartment below flight deck in glazed nose. Quick configuration changes may be made by means of modules each of which can accommodate 30 passengers in four abreast seating, litter patients and medical attendants, or cargo. Three such modules may be carried, these being loaded through the rear doors by means of overhead travelling cranes.

Status: First of four prototypes flown on 25 March 1971, with production deliveries to both Aeroflot and the Soviet Air Forces following in 1974. More than 50 in service with former and 270 with latter by beginning of 1988, when production was continuing at approximately 30 annually.

Notes: Since introduction of the basic Il-76, developed versions have included the Il-76T with additional fuel tankage, the military Il-76M (Candid-B), and the improved Il-76TD and MD. A flight refuelling tanker variant has been assigned the reporting name Midas by NATO.

ILYUSHIN IL-76 (CANDID)

Dimensions: Span, 165 ft 8$\frac{1}{3}$ in (50,50 m); length, 152 ft 10$\frac{1}{4}$ in (46,59 m); height, 48 ft 5$\frac{1}{5}$ in (14,76 m); wing area, 3,229·2 sq ft (300,00 m²).

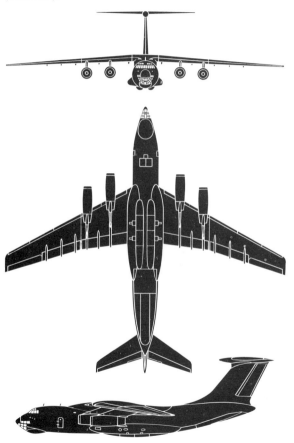

ILYUSHIN IL-86 (CAMBER)

Country of Origin: USSR.

Type: Medium-haul commercial airliner.

Power Plant: Four 28,660 lb st (13 000 kgp) Kuznetsov NK-86 turbofans.

Performance: Max cruise speed, 590 mph (950 km/h) at 29,530 ft (9 000 m); econ cruise, 559 mph (900 km/h) at 36,090 ft (11 000 m); range (with 88,185-lb/40 000-kg payload), 2,235 mls (3 600 km), (with max fuel), 2,858 mls (4 600 km).

Weights: Max take-off, 454,150 lb (206 000 kg).

Accommodation: Flight crew of three (with optional fourth member) and up to 350 passengers nine-abreast with two aisles and divided between three cabins (111, 141 and 98 seats respectively). Typical mixed-class arrangement provides for 28 passengers six-abreast in forward cabin and 206 passengers eight-abreast in centre and rear cabins.

Status: First of two prototypes flown on 22 December 1976, with deliveries (to Aeroflot) commencing in 1980, with some 60–70 delivered by beginning of 1988 when production was continuing at a rate of two monthly.

Notes: The first Soviet wide-bodied airliner, the Il-86 is operated solely by Aeroflot. Responsibility for the manufacture of the wing, stabiliser and engine pylons is invested in the Polish WSK-Mielec concern, which, according to Polish sources, had delivered 130 sets of components by mid-1985. It is generally believed that performance of the Il-86 has fallen short of expectations, and although Soviet sources claim that the newer Il-96-300 (see pages 130–1) is complementary to the Il-86, Aeroflot requirements for the latter have apparently been scaled down pending availability of the later and longer-ranging aircraft.

ILYUSHIN IL-86 (CAMBER)

Dimensions: Span, 157 ft 8⅛ in (48,06 m); length, 195 ft 4 in (59,54 m); height, 51 ft 10½ in (15,81 m); wing area, 3,550 sq ft (329,80 m²).

ILYUSHIN IL-96-300

Country of Origin: USSR.

Type: Long-haul commercial airliner.

Power Plant: Four 35,280 lb st (16 000 kgp) Soloviev D-90A turbofans.

Performance: (Estimated) Max cruise speed, 559 mph (900 km/h) at 39,370 ft (12 000 m); econ cruise, 528 mph (850 km/h); range (with 88,185-lb/40 000-kg payload), 4,660 mls (7 500 km), (with 66,140-lb/30 000-kg payload), 5,592 mls (9 000 km), (with 33,070-lb/15 000-kg payload), 6,835 mls (11 000 km).

Weights: Empty, 257,936 lb (117 000 kg); max take-off, 507,055 lb (230 000 kg).

Accommodation: Flight crew of three with typical mixed-class arrangement for 22 first class, 40 business class and 173 tourist class passengers, or all-tourist class arrangement for 300 passengers in three rows three abreast. Max capacity for 350 passengers.

Status: First Il-96-300 scheduled to commence flight test during first half of 1988. Production to proceed concurrently with flight test programme, with service entry (Aeroflot) during 1990.

Notes: Possessing close family resemblance to Il-86, the Il-96 is fundamentally a new design with supercritical wing and retaining only a common fuselage diameter with the earlier and shorter-range airliner.

ILYUSHIN IL-96-300

Dimensions: Span (excluding winglets), 189 ft 2 in (57,66 m); length, 181 ft 7¼ in (55,35 m); height, 57 ft 7¾ in (17,57 m); wing area, 3,767 sq ft (350,00 m²).

ILYUSHIN A-50 (MAINSTAY)

Country of Origin: USSR.

Type: Airborne warning and control system aircraft.

Power Plant: Four 26,455 lb st (12 000 kgp) Soloviev D-30KP turbofans.

Performance: (Estimated) Max cruise speed, 475 mph (764 km/h) at 29,500–42,650 ft (9 000–13 000 m); loiter speed, 390–410 mph (630–660 km/h) at 29,500 ft (9 000 m); time on station (unrefuelled) at 930 mls (1 500 km) from base, 6–7 hrs.

Weights: (Estimated) Max take-off, 380,000 lb (172 370 kg).

Accommodation: Probable flight crew of four with tactical and air direction teams totalling 9–10 persons.

Status: An AWACS derivative of the Il-76 (see pages 126–7), the A-50 is known to have been under test since 1979–80, initial operational capability having been attained in 1986, with some eight–nine being in service by 1988.

Notes: Successor to the Tu-126 *Moss* in service with the Soviet Voyska PVO home defence force and referred to as the A-50 (when evaluated by an Indian Air Force team), this AWACS aircraft is based on the Il-76 transport, but apparently incorporates some fuselage stretch ahead of the wings. It is said by the US Department of Defense to be capable of detecting aircraft and cruise missiles flying at low altitude over either land or water, and to be intended to assist in the direction of fighter operations over European and Asian battlefields. The MiG-31 (see pages 164–5) is apparently optimised for operation with this aircraft, production of which is believed to be proceeding at a rate of at least five annually. The operation of Mainstay in association with Su-27 counterair fighters based on the Kola Peninsula was noted during 1987.

ILYUSHIN A-50 (MAINSTAY)

Dimensions: (Estimated) Span, 165 ft 8⅓ in (50,50 m); length, 155 ft 9 in (47,50 m); height, 48 ft 5 in (14,76 m); wing area, 3,299·2 sq ft (300,00 m²).

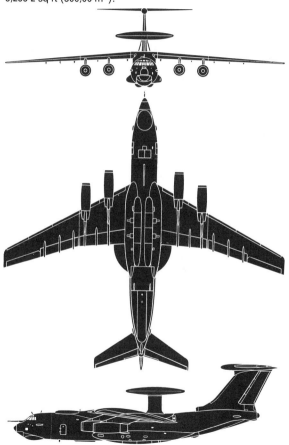

KAWASAKI T-4

Country of Origin: Japan.
Type: Tandem two-seat basic trainer.
Power Plant: Two 3,660 lb st (1 660 kgp) Ishikawajima-Harima XF3-30 turbofans.
Performance: (manufacturer's estimated) Max speed, 576 mph (927 km/h) at sea level, or Mach=0·75, 616 mph (990 km/h) at 25,000 ft (7 620 m), or Mach=0·9; max cruise, 506 mph (815 km/h) at 30,000 ft (9 145 m); max initial climb, 10,000 ft/min (50,8 m/sec); service ceiling, 40,000 ft (12 200 m); range (internal fuel), 863 mls (1 390 km).
Weights: Empty, 8,157 lb (3 700 kg); normal loaded, 12,125 lb (5 500 kg); max take-off, 16,535 lb (7 500 kg).
Armament: (Training) One 7,6-mm machine gun pod on fuselage station and one AIM-9L Sidewinder AAM on each of two wing stations, or up to four 500-lb (227 kg) practice bombs.
Status: The first of four XT-4 prototypes was flown on 29 July 1985, and the fourth was delivered to the Defence Agency in July 1986. Series production of the T-4 commenced during 1987, with initial deliveries to the Air Self-Defence Force being scheduled to commence mid-1988, procurement being expected to total some 200 aircraft.
Notes: Intended as a replacement for the Fuji T-1, the T-4 has been developed jointly by Kawasaki (as prime contractor), Mitsubishi and Fuji. Kawasaki produces the front fuselage and is responsible for final assembly. Mitsubishi manufacturing the centre and rear fuselage, the engine air intakes and vertical tail, and Fuji contributing the wings, horizontal tail surfaces, rear fuselage and cockpit canopy. The T-4 is the first Japanese aircraft to combine a nationally-designed power plant with an indigenous airframe for 25 years.

KAWASAKI T-4

Dimensions: Span, 32 ft 6 in (9,90 m); length, 42 ft 8 in 13,00 m); height, 15 ft 1 in (4,60 m); wing area, 232·5 sq ft (21,60 m²).

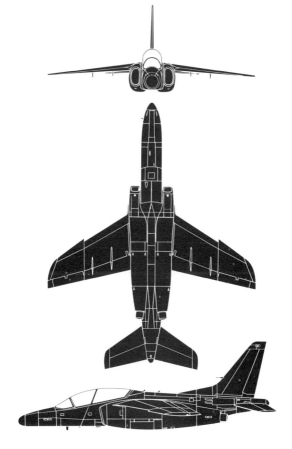

LET L-610

Country of Origin: Czechoslovakia.
Type: Short-haul regional airliner.
Power Plant: Two 1,822 shp Motorlet M 602 turboprops.
Performance: (Manufacturer's estimates) Max cruise speed, 304 mph (490 km/h) at 23,620 ft (7 200 m); long-range cruise, 253 mph (408 km/h) at 23,620 ft (7 200 m); max initial climb, 1,870 ft/min (9,5 m/sec); service ceiling, 33,630 ft (10 250 m); range (max payload and 45 min reserves), 540 mls (870 km), (max fuel), 1,495 mls (2 406 km).
Weights: (Manufacturer's estimates) Operational empty, 19,246 lb (8 730 kg); max take-off, 30,865 lb (14 000 kg).
Accommodation: Flight crew of two and standard arrangement for 40 passengers four abreast with central aisle.
Status: First of three prototypes (one static and two flying) scheduled to enter test during 1988, with certification and initial customer deliveries in 1990.
Notes: The L-610 has been designed for short-haul operations over stage lengths of 250–375 miles (400–600 km) and is intended to complement the smaller L-410 light transport (see 1986 edition) which has been in continuous production in successive versions since 1970. Although of basically similar configuration to the earlier aircraft, the L-610 possesses no commonality with the L-410. The Soviet Union is expected to be the major customer for the L610. The undercarriage of the L 610 has been designed for soft field operation and for the descent rates demanded by 'difficult' strips.

LET L-610

Dimensions: Span, 84 ft 0 in (25,60 m); length, 70 ft 3¼ in (21,42 m); height, 24 ft 11½ in (7,61 m); wing area, 602·8 sq ft (56,00 m²).

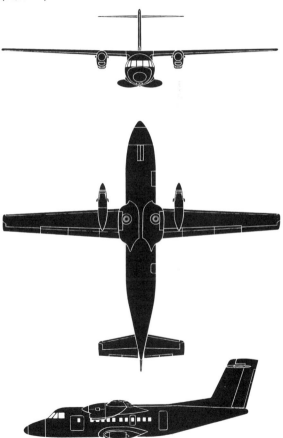

LOCKHEED C-5B GALAXY

Country of Origin: USA.
Type: Heavy strategic transport.
Power Plant: Four 41,000 lb st (18 643 kgp) General Electric TF39-GE-1C turbofans.
Performance: Max speed, 571 mph (919 km/h) at 25,000 ft (7 620 m); max cruise, 552–564 mph (888–908 km/h) at 25,000 ft (7 620 m); econ cruise, 518 mph (833 km/h); max initial climb, 1,725 ft/min (8,75 m/sec); range (with max payload), 2,728 mls (4 390 km), (max fuel and reserves), 6,850 mls (11 024 km).
Weights: Operational empty, 374,000 lb (169 643 kg); max take-off, 769,000 lb (348 820 kg).
Accommodation: Flight crew of five plus 15 seats on flight deck, 75 seats in aft troop compartment and up to 270 troops on pallet-mounted seats in cargo compartment. Up to 36 standard 463L cargo pallets, or various vehicles.
Status: First flight of C-5B took place on 10 September 1985 and first delivery to USAF followed on 8 January 1986. Total requirement for 50 aircraft of which 22 delivered during 1986–7. Production peaked in January 1988 at two per month with the 23rd aircraft, and the 50th and last aircraft is scheduled to be delivered by early 1989.
Notes: Production of 81 examples of the C-5A was completed in May 1973, manufacture of the Galaxy being reinstated in 1982 with the C-5B. Although external aerodynamic configuration and internal arrangements remain unchanged, the C-5B differs in respect of some items of equipment and incorporates from the outset various significant improvements already made on or proposed for the rewinged C-5As, all 77 of which had passed through the rewinging programme by July 1987. Apart from a new wing, the C-5B features engines of increased thrust, state-of-the-art avionics and carbon brakes.

LOCKHEED C-5B GALAXY

Dimensions: Span, 222 ft 8½ in (67,88 m); length, 247 ft 10 in (75,53 m); height, 65 ft 1½ in (19,34 m); wing area, 6,200 sq ft (575,98 m²).

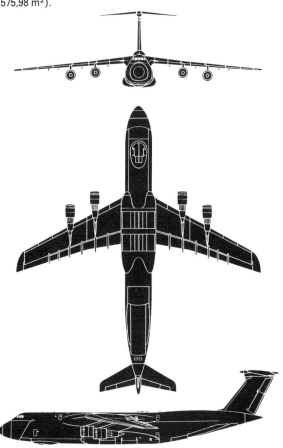

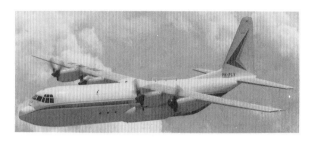

LOCKHEED L-100-30 HERCULES

Country of Origin: USA.

Type: Medium/long-range military and commercial freight transport.

Power Plant: Four 4,508 ehp Allison T56-A-15 turboprops.

Performance: Max cruise speed, 386 mph (620 km/h) at 20,000 ft (6 095 m); long-range cruise, 345 mph (556 km/h); range (max payload), 2,300 mls (3 700 km); ferry range (with 2,265 Imp gal/10 296 l of external fuel), 5,354 mls (8 617 km).

Weights: Operational empty, 79,516 lb (36 086 kg); max take-off, 155,000 lb (70 310 kg).

Accommodation: Normal flight crew of four and provision for 97 casualty litters plus medical attendants, 128 combat troops or 92 paratroops. For pure freight role up to seven cargo pallets may be loaded.

Status: A total of 1,832 Hercules (all versions) had been delivered by the beginning of 1988 when production was continuing at three monthly. One hundred and five Hercules supplied for commercial operation.

Notes: The L-100-30 and its military equivalent, the C-130H-30, are stretched versions of the basic Hercules, the C-130H. The original civil model, the L-100-20 featured a 100-in (2,54-m) fuselage stretch over the basic military model, and the L-100-30, intended for both military and civil application, embodies a further 80-in (2,03-m) stretch. Military operators of the C-130H-30 version are France, Algeria, Indonesia, Ecuador, Cameroun and Nigeria, and 30 of the RAF's Hercules C Mk 1s (equivalent of the C-130H) have been modified to C-130H-30 standards as Hercules C Mk 3s. Some 40 variants of the Hercules have so far been produced and this type now serves (in military and civil roles) with 57 countries.

LOCKHEED L-100-30 HERCULES

Dimensions: Span, 132 ft 7 in (40,41 m); length, 112 ft 9 in (34,37 m); height, 38 ft 3 in (11,66 m); wing area, 1,745 sq ft (162,12 m²).

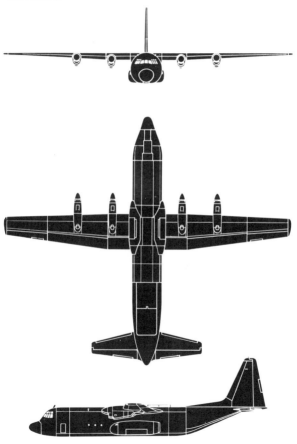

LOCKHEED P-3C ORION

Country of Origin: USA.

Type: Long-range maritime patrol aircraft.

Power Plant: Four 4,910 eshp Allison T56-A-14W turboprops.

Performance: Max speed (at 105,000 lb/47 625 kg), 473 mph (761 km/h) at 15,000 ft (4 570 m); cruise, 397 mph (639 km/h) at 25,000 ft (7 620 m); patrol speed, 230 mph (370 km/h) at 1,500 ft (460 m); loiter endurance (all engines) at 1,500 ft (460 m), 12·3 hrs, (two engines), 17 hrs; mission radius 2,530 mls (4 075 km), (with three hours on station at 1,500 ft/460 m), 1,933 mls (3 110 km).

Weights: Empty, 61,491 lb (27 890 kg); normal loaded, 133,500 lb (60 558 kg); max overload take-off, 142,000 lb (64 410 kg).

Accommodation: Normal flight crew of 10 including five in tactical compartment.

Armament: Two Mk 101 depth bombs and four Mk 43, 44 or 46 torpedoes, or eight Mk 54 bombs in weapons bay, and provision for up to 13,713 lb (6 220 kg) of external ordnance.

Status: Prototype (YP-3C) flown 8 October 1968, with deliveries to the US Navy (of P-3C Update III) continuing at beginning of 1988 against total requirement of 287 (P-3Cs) and under licence (by Kawasaki) for Japanese Maritime Self-Defence Force against total requirement for 100 aircraft.

Notes: The P-3C followed 157 P-3As and 125 P-3Bs, and has been supplied to the RAAF (20), Iran (six as P-3Fs), the Canadian Armed Forces (18 as CP-140 Auroras) and the Netherlands (13), in addition to Japan. Deliveries of the current Update III version began in May 1984, and Update IV avionics are to be installed in 133 P-3Cs. The US Navy plans procurement of 125 P-3Ds with Update IV avionics, later engines, two-crew cockpit and elongated weapons bay.

LOCKHEED P-3C ORION

Dimensions: Span, 99 ft 8 in (30,37 m); length, 116 ft 10 in (35,61 m); height, 33 ft 8½ in (10,29 m); wing area, 1,300 sq ft (120,77 m²).

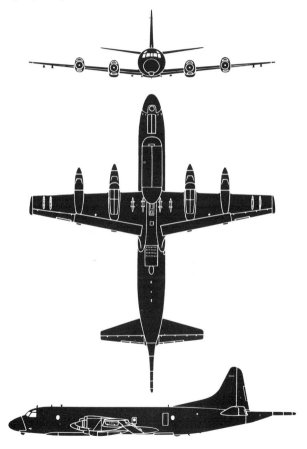

LOCKHEED P-3 SENTINEL

Country of Origin: USA.
Type: Airborne warning and control system aircraft.
Power Plant: Four 4,910 ehp Allison T56-A-14 turboprops.
Performance: Max cruising speed, 410 mph (660 km/h) at 15,000 ft (4 570 m); econ cruise, 373 mph (600 km/h) at 25,000 ft (7 620 m); average loiter speed, 240 mph (386 km/h) at 25,000 ft (7 620 m); time on station (unrefuelled), 8·5 hrs at 920 mls (1 480 km) from base; max range, 4,836 mls (7 783 km); max endurance, 14 hrs.
Weights: Empty, 68,554 lb (31 096 kg); max take-off, 134,770 lb (61 132 kg).
Accommodation: Flight crew of four and tactical team of four plus provision for relief personnel, or tactical team of 7–10 plus relief personnel according to equipment.
Status: Prototype (converted from P-3B) first flown on 13 June 1984. One ordered by US Customs Service in June 1987, with an option on three additional aircraft. First aircraft to fly with full radar summer 1988, with delivery early 1989.
Notes: A derivative of the P-3 Orion maritime patrol and ASW aircraft (see pages 142–3), the P-3 Sentinel is being proposed with various levels of equipment sophistication. The version for the US Customs Service, which is to be used for the surveillance of the main drug-smuggling routes, is a relatively simple aircraft with an APS-125 search radar, but there is an option to fit the later APS-145 when it becomes available late 1989. More sophisticated versions of the aircraft with much enhanced capability are being offered to current operators of the maritime patrol P-3.

LOCKHEED P-3 SENTINEL

Dimensions: Span, 99 ft 8 in (30,37 m); length, 107 ft 7$\frac{1}{3}$ in (32,80 m); height, 33 ft 8$\frac{1}{2}$ in (10,27 m); wing area, 1,300 sq ft (120,77 m²).

LTV YA-7F CORSAIR II

Country of Origin: USA.

Type: Single-seat attack and close air support aircraft.

Power Plant: One 14,375 lb st (6 520 kgp) dry and 23,830 lb st (10 809 kgp) reheat Pratt & Whitney F100-PW-220 turbofan.

Performance: (Estimated) Max speed (clean), 803 mph (1 292 km/h) at 10,000 ft (3 050 m), or Mach = 1·1, (with two MK 84 bombs, LANA and ECM pods, two AIM-9 missiles and 50 per cent fuel), 715 mph (1 151 km/h) at 10,000 ft (3 050 m), or Mach = 0·98; combat radius, 770 mls (1 240 km) HI-LO-HI, 334 mls (537 km) LO-LO-LO.

Weights: Max take-off, 46,000 lb (20 866 kg).

Armament: One 20-mm M-61A-1 Vulcan rotary cannon and (for typical HI-LO-HI mission) six 500-lb (227-kg) Mk 82 bombs and two AIM-9 AAMs distributed between two fuselage-side and six wing stations. Max ordnance load, 17,380 lb (7 883 kg).

Status: Two YA-7Fs (rebuilt A-7Ds) are scheduled to enter flight test during course of 1988, with delivery to USAF for evaluation in following year.

Notes: The YA-7F is a rebuilt and extensively upgraded version of the A-7D, and it is proposed to similarly modify 330 plus Air National Guard A-7Ds as interim close air support and interdiction aircraft for service from the early 'nineties until about 2010. The YA-7F embodies a 47·5-in (1,20-m) fuselage stretch and its engine bay can accommodate the General Electric F110-GE-100 as an alternative to the F100-PW-220. The LANA (Low Altitude Night Attack) pod will be carried, a taller fin is fitted and the wing has new augmented flaps and lift spoilers.

LTV YA-7F CORSAIR II

Dimensions: Span, 38 ft 9 in (11,80 m); length, 50 ft 1½ in (15,27 m); height, 16 ft 0¾ in (4,90 m); wing area, 375 sq ft (34,83 m²).

McDONNELL DOUGLAS F-15E EAGLE

Country of Origin: USA.

Type: Two-seat dual-role (air-air and air-ground) fighter.

Power Plant: Two 14,370 lb st (6 518 kgp) dry and 23,450 lb st (10 637 kgp) reheat Pratt & Whitney F100-PW-220 turbofans.

Performance: Max speed (short-endurance dash), 1,676 mph (2 698 km/h), or Mach = 2·54, (sustained), 1,518 mph (2 443 km/h), or Mach = 2·3, at 40,000 ft (12 190 m); service ceiling, 60,000 ft (18 300 m); ferry range (with conformal tanks and max external fuel), 3,570 mls (5 745 km).

Weights: Basic operational empty, 31,700 lb (14 379 kg); max take-off, 81,000 lb (36 741 kg).

Armament: One 20-mm M61A1 six-barrel rotary cannon and (air-air) up to four each AIM-7F Sparrow and AIM-9L Sidewinder AAMs, or up to eight AIM-120 AAMs, or (air-ground) up to 23,500 lb (10 659 kg) of ordnance on wing and fuselage stations plus tangential carriers on conformal tanks.

Status: First production F-15E flown on 11 December 1986. USAF requirement for 392 aircraft of this type with initial operational capability from late 1988.

Notes: A derivative of the basic Eagle (see 1986 edition) for long-range, deep interdiction and high-ordnance-load air-ground missions by day, night or in adverse weather, the F-15E embodies a restressed and strengthened structure affording double the life of earlier Eagles, engine bays tailored to accept either the F100 or the General Electric F110 engine, and a triplex digital (fly-by-wire) flight control system. Current production versions of the Eagle in addition to the F-15E are the single-seat F-15C air superiority fighter and its tandem two-seat operational training equivalent, the F-15D.

McDONNELL DOUGLAS F-15E EAGLE

Dimensions: Span, 42 ft 9¾ in (13,05 m); length, 63 ft 9 in (19,43 m); height, 18 ft 5½ in (5,63 m); wing area, 608 sq ft (56,50 m²).

McDONNELL DOUGLAS F/A-18 HORNET

Country of Origin: USA.
Type: Single-seat shipboard and shore-based multi-role fighter and attack aircraft.
Power Plant: Two 10,600 lb st (4 810 kgp) dry and 15,800 lb st (7 167 kgp) reheat General Electric F404-GE-400 turbofans.
Performance: Max speed (AAMs on wingtip and fuselage stations), 1,190 mph (1 915 km/h) or Mach=1·8 at 40,000 ft (12 150 m); initial climb (half fuel and wingtip AAMs), 60,000 ft/min (304,6 m/sec); tactical radius (combat air patrol on internal fuel), 480 mls (770 km), (with three 262 Imp gal/1 192 l external tanks), 735 mls (1 180 km).
Weights: Empty equipped, 28,000 lb (12 700 kg); loaded (air superiority mission with half fuel and four AAMs), 35,800 lb (16 240 kg); max take-off, 56,000 lb (25 400 kg).
Armament: One 20-mm M-61A-1 rotary cannon and (air-air) two AIM-7E/F Sparrow and two AIM-9G/H Sidewinder AAMs, or (attack) up to 17,000 lb (7 711 kg) of ordnance.
Status: First of 11 FSD (full-scale development) Hornets (including two TF-18A two-seaters) flown 18 November 1978. Planning at beginning of 1988 called for 1,150 Hornets for US Navy and US Marine Corps. First production F/A-18A flown April 1980, and first F/A-18C on 3 September 1987. Some 570 delivered by beginning of 1988.
Notes: Land-based versions of the Hornet have been ordered by Australia (57 F/A-18As and 18 TF-18As), Canada (113 CF-18As and 24 CF-18Bs) and Spain (72 EF-18As and TF-18As). Separate F-18 fighter and A-18 attack versions of the Hornet initially planned, but roles subsequently combined in a single basic version. The F/A-18C (illustrated) embodies some new systems and has provision for the AIM-132 and AGM-65D missiles. The two-seat equivalent is the F/A-18D.

McDONNEL DOUGLAS F/A-18 HORNET

Dimensions: Span, 37 ft 6 in (11,43 m); length, 56 ft 0 in (17,07 m); height, 15 ft 4 in (4,67 m); wing area, 396 sq ft (36,79 m²).

McDONNELL DOUGLAS KC-10A EXTENDER

Country of Origin: USA.

Type: Flight refuelling tanker and military freighter.

Power Plant: Three 52,500 lb st (23 814 kgp) General Electric CF6-50C2 turbofans.

Performance: Max speed, 620 mph (988 km/h) at 33,000 ft (10 060 m); max cruise, 595 mph (957 km/h) at 31,000 ft (9 450 m); long-range cruise, 540 mph (870 km/h); typical refuelling mission, 2,200 mls (3 540 km) from base with 200,000 lb (90 720 kg) of fuel and return; max range (with 170,000 lb/77 112 kg freight), 4,370 mls (7 033 km).

Weights: Operational empty (tanker), 239,747 lb (108 749 kg), (cargo configuration), 243,973 lb (110 660 kg); max take-off, 590,000 lb (267 624 kg).

Accommodation: Flight crew of five plus provision for six seats for additional crew and four bunks for crew rest. Fourteen further seats may be provided for support personnel in the forward cabin. Alternatively, a larger area can be provided for 55 more support personnel, with necessary facilities, to increase total accommodation (including flight crew) to 80.

Status: First KC-10A was flown on 12 July 1980, with first operational squadron activated on 1 October 1981. The 60th and last KC-10A ordered by the USAF will be completed during 1988 and delivered in 1989.

Notes: The KC-10A is a military tanker/freighter derivative of the commercial DC-10 Series 30 (see 1983 edition). The 60th aircraft is to be fitted with two additional hosedrogue refuelling systems in wing pods, permitting three probe-equipped aircraft to be refuelled simultaneously. All remaining 59 aircraft of the fleet will be similarly modified.

McDONNELL DOUGLAS KC-10A EXTENDER

Dimensions: Span, 165 ft 4 in (50,42 m); length, 182 ft 0 in (55,47 m); height, 58 ft 1 in (17,70 m); wing area, 3,958 sq ft (367,7 m²).

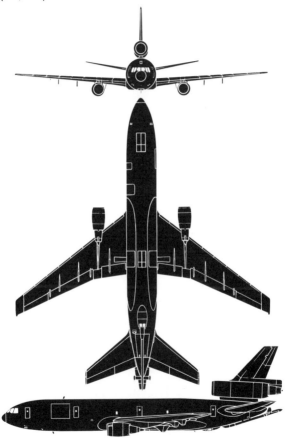

McDONNELL DOUGLAS/BAe T-45A GOSHAWK

Country of Origin: USA (United Kingdom).

Type: Tandem two-seat carrier-capable basic/advanced trainer.

Power Plant: One 5,450 lb st (2 472 kgp) Rolls-Royce Turboméca F405-RR-400L (Adour Mk 861-49) turbofan.

Performance: Max speed, 609 mph (980 km/h) at 8,000 ft (2 440 m), or Mach=0·85; max initial climb, 6,740 ft/min (34,24 m/sec); time to 30,000 ft (9 145 m), 6·88 min; service ceiling, 42,500 ft (12 955 m); ferry range, 1,151 mls (1 853 km), (with two 156 US gal/591 l external tanks), 1,819 mls (2 928 km).

Weights: Empty, 9,335 lb (4 234 kg); max take-off, 12,851 lb (5 829 kg).

Status: First and second prototypes of the T-45A scheduled to fly early 1988. The US Navy has a requirement for 302 T-45As of which first three production lots (totalling 60 aircraft) were contracted for on 23 May 1986, and annual purchase of 48 is planned 1991–1995. Initial operational capability (with 12 aircraft) to be attained in September 1990.

Notes: The T-45A Goshawk is derived from the BAe Hawk (see pages 54–5) and will be part of an integrated training system (T-45TS) embodying aircraft, academics, simulators and logistics support. Seventy-six per cent of manufacture is being undertaken in the USA, and differences to the Hawk include addition of arrester hook, relocated air brakes, revised undercarriage, changes to wing movable surfaces and provision of catapult nose-tow launch assemblies.

McDONNELL DOUGLAS/BAe T-45A GOSHAWK

Dimensions: Span, 30 ft 9¾ in (9,39 m); length (including probe), 39 ft 3⅛ in (11,97 m); height, 13 ft 6⅛ in (4,12 m); wing area, 179·64 sq ft (16,69 m²).

McDONNELL DOUGLAS MD-87

Country of Origin: USA.

Type: Short-to-medium-haul commercial airliner.

Power Plant: Two 20,860 lb st (9 462 kgp) Pratt & Whitney JT8D-217B/C turbofans.

Performance: Max cruise speed, 575 mph (925 km/h) at 27,000 ft (8 230 m); econ cruise, 522 mph (840 km/h) at 33,000 ft (10 060 m); range cruise, 505 mph (813 km/h) at 35,000 ft (10 670 m); range (max payload), 2,144 mls (3 450 km), (max fuel), 3,405 mls (5 480 km).

Weights: Operational empty, 73,157 lb (33 253 kg); max take-off, 140,000 lb (63 500 kg).

Accommodation: Flight crew of two and max single-class seating for 115–139 passengers five abreast with optional mixed-class arrangements to suit customer requirements.

Status: The first MD-87 entered flight test on 4 December 1986, with first customer deliveries (to Austrian and Finnair) October 1987. Orders for all versions of the MD-80 series (including conditional orders and options) totalled 845 by January 1988, with 442 delivered and production continuing at approximately eight per month.

Notes: The MD-87 is the smallest member of the MD-80 family, the fuselage being 17·4 ft (5,30 m) shorter than other airliners in the series (ie, MD-81, -82, -83 and -88) which differ primarily in weight and power plant, the MD-88 being essentially an MD-82 with an advanced cockpit. All the MD-80 family use the same wing and are available with any of the JT8D-200 series of engines. The MD-80 series is being co-produced in China, 25 MD-82s initially being partially assembled in the USA before shipment to China for completion by the Shanghai Aviation Industrial Corporation.

McDONNELL DOUGLAS MD-87

Dimensions: Span, 107 ft 10 in (32,85 m); length, 130 ft 5 in (39,75 m); height, 30 ft 6 in (9,30 m); wing area, 1,270 sq ft (117,98 m²).

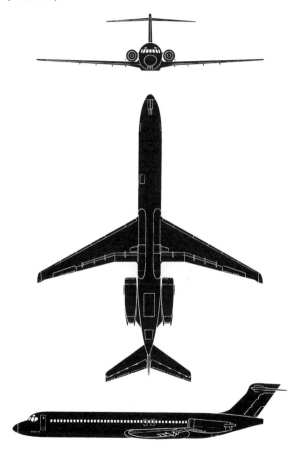

McDONNELL DOUGLAS TAV-8B HARRIER II

Country of Origin: USA and United Kingdom.
Type: Tandem two-seat conversion trainer.
Power Plant: One 21,450 lb st (9 730 kgp) Rolls Royce F402-RR-406 vectored-thrust turbofan.
Performance: Max speed, 667 mph (1 074 km/h) at sea level, or Mach = 0·87, 587 mph (945 km/h) at altitude, or Mach = 0·9; ferry range (with two 300 US gal/1 136 l external tanks retained), 1,647 mls (2 650 km).
Weights: Operational empty, 14,221 lb (6 451 kg); max take-off (for STO), 29,750 lb (13 495 kg).
Armament: Two twin-store wing stations for four LAU-68 rocket launchers or six Mk 76 practice bombs.
Status: First of 28 TAV-8Bs for US Marine Corps flown on 21 October 1986, with service entry having commenced mid 1987.
Notes: The TAV-8B is a two-seat instructional derivative of the single-seat AV-8B close support aircraft which also serves with the RAF as the Harrier GR Mk 5 (see pages 52–53). Developed by McDonnell Douglas, with British Aerospace as sub-contractor, the TAV-8B features a new forward fuselage and canopy, and new vertical tail surfaces, but is, in other respects, similar to the AV-8B, retaining the centre and aft fuselage, wing, cockpit, avionics and power plant of the single-seater. The seats for pupil and instructor are vertically staggered, and the pupil's cockpit reproduces that of the single-seat AV-8B. The handling characteristics of the two-seater are alleged to be almost identical to those of the single-seater. The TAV-8B has replaced the British-built TAV-8A Harrier in service with the US Marine Corps V/STOL training squadron, VMAT-203, at Cherry Point, North Carolina, from late 1987, and is being utilised for both pilot and weapon training. The TAV-8B does not possess secondary combat capability.

McDONNELL DOUGLAS TAV-8B HARRIER II

Dimensions: Span, 30 ft 4 in (9,24 m); length, 50 ft 6 in (15,39 m); height, 13 ft 4¾ in (4,08 m); wing area, 238·4 sq ft (22,15 m²).

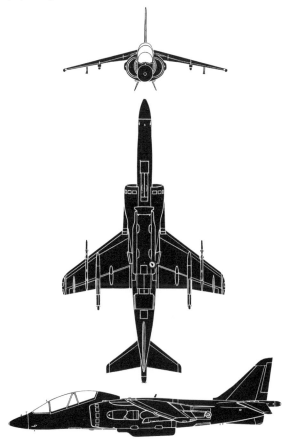

MIKOYAN MIG-27M (FLOGGER-J)

Country of Origin: USSR.

Type: Single-seat tactical strike and close support fighter.

Power Plant: One 17,675 lb st (8 020 kgp) dry and 25,350 lb st (11 500 kgp) reheat Tumansky R-29-300 turbojet.

Performance: Max speed (clean aircraft with 50% fuel), 685 mph (1 102 km/h) at 1,000 ft (305 m), or Mach=0.95, 1,056 mph (1 700 km/h) at 36,090 ft (11 000 m), or Mach=1·6; combat radius (LO-LO-LO with two 1,100-lb/500-kg bombs and two AS-14 AGMs, plus GSh-23L gun pod), 242 mls (390 km); ferry range (max external fuel), 1,553 mls (2 500 km).

Weights: Empty, 23,850 lb (10 818 kg); max take-off, 39,685 lb (18 000 kg).

Armament: One 23-mm six-barrel rotary cannon and up to 6,614 lb (3 00 kg) of ordnance distributed between seven stores stations (five on fuselage and two on wing glove).

Status: Derived from the MiG-23 (see 1987 edition) as a dedicated air-ground aircraft, the MiG-27 entered service (in Flogger-D form) in 1975–76, with production continuing at beginning of 1987 in both Soviet Union and India where licence manufacture of 165 (Flogger-J) is being undertaken.

Notes: The MiG-27 has a basically similar forward fuselage to that of the Flogger-F and -H minimum-change air-ground derivatives of the MiG-23 counterair fighter, but is more closely tailored for subsonic ground attack operations, with additional armour, rough-field undercarriage and modified engine with fixed-geometry air intakes. The MiG-27M features lengthened nose and wing leading-edge extensions by comparison with earlier production series. Deliveries to the Indian Air Force (from CKD assemblies) commenced mid 1985.

MIKOYAN MIG-27M (FLOGGER-J)

Dimensions: (Estimated) Span (17deg sweep), 46 ft 9 in (14,25 m), (72 deg sweep), 26 ft 9 in (8,17 m); length, 54 ft 1⅔ in (16,50 m): height, 14 ft 9 in (4,50 m); wing area, 293·4 sq ft (27,26 m²).

MIKOYAN MIG-29 (FULCRUM-A)

Country of Origin: USSR.

Type: Single-seat counterair fighter.

Power Plant: Two 11,243 lb st (5 100 kgp) dry and 18,300 lb st (8 300 kgp) reheat Tumansky R-33D turbofans.

Performance: (Estimated) Max speed (with four AAMs and half fuel), 1,518 mph (2 445 km/h) above 36,100 ft (11 000 m), or Mach = 2·3, 915 mph (1 470 km/h) at sea level, or Mach = 1·2; max initial climb, 50,000 ft/min (254 m/sec); combat radius (air-air mission with four AAMs), 415 mls (670 km), (subsonic area intercept with external fuel), 715 mls (1 150 km).

Weights: (Estimated) Operational empty, 18,000 lb (8 165 kg); max take-off, 36,000 lb (16 330 kg).

Armament: One 30-mm rotary cannon plus four R-60 Aphid or AA-11 Archer close-range AAMs and two R-23R Apex or AA-10 Alamo medium-range AAMs. Four 1,100 lb (500 kg) bombs for secondary attack mission.

Status: Reportedly first flown in prototype form in 1978, the MiG-29 attained initial operational capability with the Soviet Air Forces in 1984, and about 350–400 were expected to be in service by the beginning of 1988. Forty-five (including two-seaters) were supplied to the Indian Air Force from December 1986, and India has an option to build a further 110 under licence. First deliveries to Syria were effected early 1987.

Notes: Of fundamentally similar configuration to the larger and heavier Su-27 (see pages 202–3), the MiG-29 features long-range track-while-scan radar, and pulse-Doppler look-down/shootdown weapon system, infrared search and tracking, and a digital data link. The initial service version of the MiG-29 had ventral tail fins (*à la* Su-27), these subsequently being discarded.

MIKOYAN MIG-29 (FULCRUM-A)

Dimensions: (Estimated) Span, 37 ft 9 in (11·50 m); length (including probe), 56 ft 5 in (17,20 m); height, 14 ft 9 in (4,50 m).

MIKOYAN MIG-31 (FOXHOUND)

Country of Origin: USSR.
Type: Tandem two-seat interceptor fighter.
Power Plant: Two 30,865 lb st (14 000 kgp) reheat Tumansky R-31F turbojets.
Performance: (Estimated) Max speed, 1,520 mph (2 445 km/h) above 36,100 ft (11 000 m), or Mach = 2·3; max operational radius (with external fuel), 1,180 mls (1 900 km); ceiling, 80,000 ft (24 385 m).
Weights: (Estimated) Empty equipped, 47,000 lb (21,320 kg); normal loaded, 65,200 lb (29 575 kg); max take-off, 77,160 lb (35 000 kg).
Armament: Up to eight AA-9 Amos semi-active radar-homing long-range AAMs (four on fuselage stations and four on wing stations), or mix of four AA-9s and four short-range missiles such as AA-8 Aphid, or AA-11 Archer.
Status: The MiG-31 is known to have been under development since the mid 'seventies and is believed to have been first deployed by a Voiska PVO air defence regiment in 1983. Some 160 were believed to be in service by the beginning of 1988, production being centred at Gorkiy.
Notes: Although the design of the MiG-31 is fundamentally based on that of the late 'sixties vintage MiG-25 (see 1984 edition), it differs from its predecessor in a number of respects, notably in having an entirely redesigned two-seat forward fuselage, pilot and weapon systems operator being seated in tandem. It possesses a lookdown/shootdown pulse-Doppler weapons system, has multiple target engagement capability and its engines are believed to be similar to those employed by the modified MiG-25, referred to as the Ye-266M, which established a series of world altitude records.

Dimensions: (Estimated) Span, 45 ft 9 in (13,94 m); length (excluding probe), 68 ft 10 in (21,00 m); height, 18 ft 6 in (5,63 m); wing area, 602·8 sq ft (56,00 m²).

NORMAN NAC 6 FIELDMASTER

Country of Origin: United Kingdom.
Type: Two-seat agricultural aircraft.
Power Plant: One 750 shp Pratt & Whitney Canada PT6A-34AG turboprop.
Performance: Cruising speed (at 10,000 lb/4 536 kg), 177 mph (285 km/h) at sea level, 163 mph (263 km/h) at 6,000 ft (1 830 m); max initial climb (at 10,000 lb/4 536 kg), 711 ft/min (3,61 m/sec); service ceiling, 15,000 ft (4 570 m); endurance (with one occupant and 4,486-lb/2 035-kg chemical load), 1·5 hrs; max range, 921 mls (1 482 km).
Weights: Empty equipped, 4,570 lb (2 154 kg); max take-off, 10,000 lb (4 536 kg).
Status: Prototype flown on 17 December 1981, with initial production aircraft flown 29 March 1987, and first customer delivery following in June. Planned monthly production rate of 1·5 aircraft from 1988.
Notes: The first agricultural aircraft designed from the outset for turboprop power, the Fieldmaster will normally be flown as a single-seater, but accommodation is provided for a second person and removable dual controls may be installed to simplify flying training and check-out procedures. The Fieldmaster is also suitable for fire-fighting duties for which it may be fitted with a fast-action water scoop. The integral titanium hopper/tank has a capacity of 520 Imp gal (2 366 l) and forms part of the primary structure, the power plant being mounted on the front of this, with the aft fuselage being attached to its rear, the wings being attached directly on each side.

NORMAN NAC 6 FIELDMASTER

Dimensions: Span, 53 ft 7 in (16,33 m); length, 36 ft 2 in (10,97 m); height, 13 ft 6 in (4,15 m); wing area, 358 sq ft (33,25 m²).

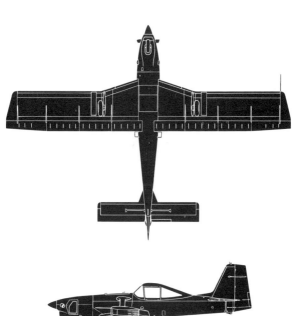

PANAVIA TORNADO F MK 3

Country of Origin: United Kingdom.

Type: Tandem two-seat air defence interceptor.

Power Plant: Two (approx) 9,000 lb st (4 082 kgp) dry and 17,000 lb st (7 711 kgp) reheat Turbo-Union RB.199-34R Mk 104 turbofans.

Performance: (Estimated) Max speed, 920 mph (1 480 km/h) or Mach = 1·2 at sea level, 1,450 mph (2 333 km/h) or Mach = 2·2 at 40,000 ft (12 190 m); time to 30,000 ft (9 145 m), 1·7 min; operational radius (combat air patrol with two 330 Imp gal/1 500 l drop tanks and allowance for 2 hrs loiter), 350–450 mls (560–725 km); ferry range (with four 330 Imp gal/1 400 l external tanks), 2,650 mls (4 265 km).

Weights: (Estimated) Empty equipped, 31,970 lb (14 500 kg); normal loaded (four Sky Flash and four AIM-9L AAMs), 50,700 lb (30 000 kg); max, 56,000 lb (25 400 kg).

Armament: One 27-mm IWKA-Mauser cannon plus four BAe Sky Flash and four AIM-9L Sidewinder AAMs.

Status: First of three F Mk 2 prototypes flown on 27 October 1979, and first of 18 production F Mk 2s (including six F Mk 2Ts) flown 5 March 1984. Deliveries of F Mk 3s (against RAF requirement for 147) commenced in 1986. Eight ordered by Oman and 24 by Saudi Arabia.

Notes: The Tornado F Mk 3 is the definitive air defence version for the RAF of the multi-national (UK, Federal Germany and Italy) multi-role fighter (see 1978 edition). It differs from the Mk 2 in having Mk 104 engines with 14-in (36-cm) reheat pipe extensions, automatic wing sweep selection, a second inertial platform and provision for four rather than two AIM-9L Sidewinders. It was anticipated at the beginning of 1988 that the F Mk 2s (illustrated above) would be reworked to F Mk 2A standard which will approximate to the F Mk 3, but will retain the earlier Mk 103 engines.

PANAVIA TORNADO F MK 3

Dimensions: Span (25 deg sweep), 45 ft 7¼ in (13,90 m), (68 deg sweep), 28 ft 2½ in (8,59 m); length, 59 ft 3 in (18,06 m); height, 18 ft 8½ in (5,70 m); wing area, 322·9 sq ft (30,00 m²).

PIAGGIO P. 180 AVANTI

Country of Origin: Italy.
Type: Light corporate transport.
Power Plant: Two 800 shp Pratt & Whitney Canada PT6A-66 turboprops.
Performance: (Manufacturer's estimates) Max speed, 460 mph (740 km/h) at 27,000 ft (8 230 m); econ cruise, 368 mph (593 km/h); max initial climb, 3,650 ft/min (18,54 m/sec); max altitude, 41,000 ft (12 500 m); range (with four passengers and NBAA reserves), 2,072 mls (3 335 km) at econ cruise.
Weights: Empty equipped, 6,700 lb (3 040 kg); max take-off, 10,509 lb (4 767 kg).
Accommodation: Pilot and co-pilot/passenger on flight deck with standard executive main cabin configuration for seven passengers in individual seats.
Status: First of two flying prototypes entered flight test on 23 September 1986, with second following on 15 May 1987. Certification anticipated late 1988, with initial customer deliveries late 1989. Initial batch of 12 commenced during 1987.
Notes: The Avanti is of innovative configuration, being of so-called 'three-surface' concept, a foreplane balancing an aft-located mainplane and a tailplane being retained for pitch control, this arrangement being claimed to result in significant aerodynamic benefits. The wing is of laminar flow section and high aspect ratio, and novel constructional methods are employed to provide an exceptionally smooth outer skin. The Avanti is primarily of metal construction, but composite parts include the foreplane, tail surfaces, engine nacelles, nose cone and some wing elements.

PIAGGIO P.180 AVANTI

Dimensions: Span, 45 ft 4⅞ in (13,84 m); length, 46 ft 5⅞ in (14,17 m); height, 12 ft 9½ in (3,90 m); wing area, 169·86 sq ft (15,78 m²).

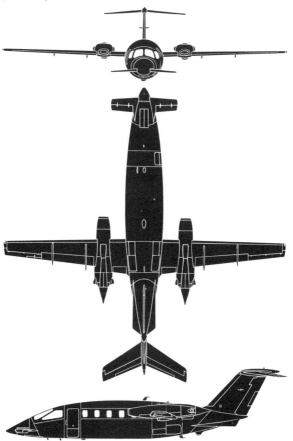

PILATUS PC-9

Country of Origin: Switzerland.
Type: Tandem two-seat basic/advanced trainer.
Power Plant: One 950 shp Pratt & Whitney Canada PT6A-62 turboprop.
Performance: Max speed, 368 mph (593 km/h) at 20,000 ft (6 100 m); max cruise, 311 mph (500 km/h) at sea level, 345 mph (556 km/h) at 20,000 ft (6 100 m); max initial climb, 4,090 ft/min (20,77 m/sec); max range (with five per cent fuel reserve plus 20 min), 690 mls (1 110 km) at 10,000 ft (3 050 m), 956 mls (1 538 km) at 20,000 ft (6 100 m).
Weights: Basic empty, 3,715 lb (1 685 kg); max take-off (aerobatic), 4,960 lb (2 250 kg), (utility), 7,055 lb (3 200 kg).
Status: First and second prototypes flown on 7 May and 20 July 1984, with first production deliveries (against an order for four from Burma) late 1985. Sixty-seven ordered by RAAF of which two delivered flyaway, six as kits and remainder being built by Hawker de Havilland. Thirty ordered by Royal Saudi Air Force, with first handed over on 15 December 1986, four ordered by Angola, and 15 for Iraq by beginning of 1988, 45 being scheduled for delivery during course of the year.
Notes: The PC-9 bears a close external resemblance to the PC-7 (see 1984 edition) of which more than 370 have been sold. It is, however, a very different aircraft, with only about 10 per cent structural commonality with the earlier trainer. The PC-9s being delivered to Saudi Arabia are supplied via British Aerospace which is responsible for the installation of cockpit instrumentation closely compatible with that of the BAe Hawk which is also being procured for the Royal Saudi Air Force.

PILATUS PC-9

Dimensions: Span, 33 ft 5 in (10,19 m); length, 32 ft 4 in (10,17 m); height, 10 ft 8⅓ in (3,26 m); wing area, 175·3 sq ft (16,29 m²).

PROMAVIA JET SQUALUS F1300 NGT

Country of Origin: Belgium (Italy).
Type: Side-by-side two-seat primary/basic trainer.
Power Plant: One 1,330 lb st (603 kgp) Garrett TFE109-1 turbofan.
Performance: (With TFE109 uprated to 1,500 lb st/680 kgp) Max speed, 363 mph (584 km/h) at 14,000 ft (4 265 m); normal operating speed, 345 mph (556 km/h); max initial climb, 3,200 ft/min (16,25 m/sec); service ceiling, 37,000 ft (11 280 m); ferry range (max internal fuel), 1,150 mls (1 853 km) at 20,000 ft (6 095 m).
Weights: Empty equipped, 2,866 lb (1 300 kg); loaded (aerobatic), 4,410 lb (2 000 kg); max take-off, 5,291 lb (2 400 kg).
Armament: (Weapons training) Provision for four wing stores stations with total capacity of 1,320 lb (600 kg).
Status: First of two prototypes flown on 30 April 1987, with second scheduled to join flight test programme May 1988. Reported options on 18 aircraft from two unspecified foreign governments by beginning of 1988 when initial production deliveries were anticipated for 1990.
Notes: The Jet Squalus (Shark) has been designed by Stelio Frati of General Avia in Italy on behalf of Promavia S.A. of Belgium in which country it is proposed that manufacture be undertaken by Sonaca S.A. The second prototype is to have uprated (1,500 lb st/680 kgp) engine and provision for cabin pressurisation. The Jet Squalus possesses the lowest airframe weight of any current pure jet trainer and its operating costs are claimed to compare favourably with those of available turboprop-powered trainers, projected acquisition cost also being comparable. The prototypes of the Jet Squalus have been built at the General Avia facility in Italy.

PROMAVIA JET SQUALUS F1300 NGT

Dimensions: Span, 29 ft 7⅞ in (9,04 m); length, 30 ft 8½ in (9,36 m); height, 11 ft 9¾ in (3,60 m); wing area, 146·18 sq ft (13,58 m²).

PZL I-22 IRYD

Country of Origin: Poland.
Type: Tandem two-seat advanced trainer and light close support aircraft.
Power Plant: Two 2,425 lb st (1 100 kgp) PZL Rzeszów SO-3W22 turbojets.
Performance: Max speed, 568 mph (915 km/h), or Mach = 0·85, at sea level; initial climb, 7,218 ft/min (36,66 m/sec); service ceiling, 41,340 ft (12 600 m).
Weights: Empty, 8,734 lb (3 962 kg); max take-off, 16,519 lb (7 493 kg).
Armament: One 23-mm twin-barrel cannon pack on fuselage centreline and four 1,100-lb (500-kg) wing hardpoints for ordnance.
Status: First of two prototypes flown on 3 March 1985, with development continuing at beginning of 1988 to fulfil a Polish Air Force requirement for a successor to the TS-11 Iskra.
Notes: The I-22 Iryd (Iridium) has been designed by the Aviation Institute at Warszawa-Okęcie to fulfil the roles of basic/advanced training and all-weather tactical strike and reconnaisance, placing emphasis on modest field requirements and ease of servicing and maintenance under comparatively primitive conditions. The prototypes have been built by the PZL Mielec facility which will be responsible for series production. No details have been revealed concerning the timescale for service entry of the Iryd to which it is assumed that Polish Air Force pilots will convert from the Orlik.

PZL I-22 IRYD

Dimensions: Span, 31 ft 5$\frac{7}{8}$ in (9,60 m); length, 43 ft 4$\frac{1}{2}$ in (13,22 m); height, 14 ft 1$\frac{1}{4}$ in (4,30 m); wing area, 214·42 sq ft (19,92 m²).

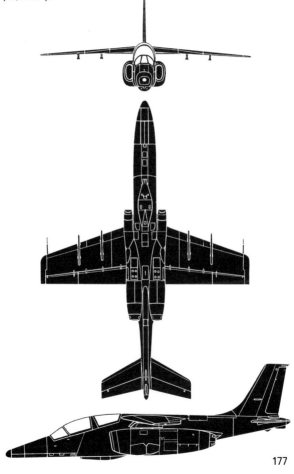

177

PZL M-26 ISKIERKA

Country of Origin: Poland.
Type: Tandem two-seat primary/basic trainer.
Power Plant: One 300 hp Textron Lycoming AEIO-540-LIB5B six-cylinder horizontally-opposed engine.
Performance: (Manufacturer's estimates) Max cruise speed, 211 mph (340 km/h) at 4,920 ft (1 500 m); max initial climb, 1,575 ft/min (8,0 m/sec); max range (with 30 min reserves), 1,007 mls (1 620 km).
Weights: Operational empty, 2,072 lb (9 40 kg); max take-off, 3,086 lb (1 400 kg).
Status: First prototype (M-26 00) flown on 18 July 1986, with second prototype (M-26 01) having been scheduled to enter flight test late 1987. No production plans announced by the beginning of 1988.
Notes: The Iskierka (Little Spark) is being developed by the WSK-PZL Mielec to FAR Part 23 airworthiness requirements, and, with the Textron Lycoming engine, is expected to be certificated in the USA. The first prototype, the M-26 00, is powered by a 205 hp PZL (Franklin) F6A350C1 engine, but development is currently concentrated on the more powerful M-26 01 which is intended for both civil and military flying training. The Iskierka embodies some components of the M-20 Mewa (Gull), a Polish version of the Piper PA-34 Seneca II, in the wings, tail assembly, undercarriage and electrical system. It is currently proposed as a successor to the PZL-110 Koliber (Humming Bird), a version of the Socata Rallye 100 ST, for use by the Aero Club of the Polish People's Republic.

Dimensions: Span, 28 ft 2⅔ in (8,60 m); length, 27 ft 2¾ in (8,30 m); height, 9 ft 8½ in (2,96 m); wing area, 150·7 sq ft (14,00 m²).

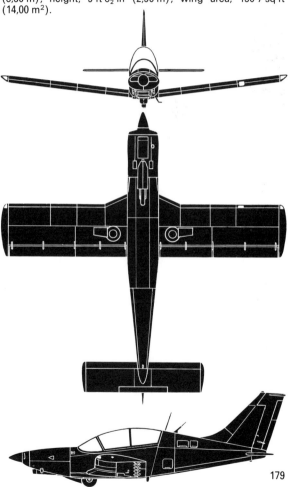

PZL-130T TURBO ORLIK

Country of Origin: Poland.
Type: Tandem two-seat basic/advanced trainer.
Power Plant: One 550 shp Pratt & Whitney Canada PT6A-25A turboprop.
Performance: (At aerobatic weight) Max speed, 310 mph (499 km/h) at 15,000 ft (4 575 m); max cruise, 272 mph (438 km/h) at sea level; max initial climb, 3,130 ft/min (15,9 m/sec); range, 694 mls (1 117 km) at 286 mph (460 km/h), 800 mls (1 287 km) at 161 mph (260 km/h), (with max external fuel), 1,343 mls (2 161 km) at 282 mph (454 km/h), 1,397 mls (2 220 km) at 169 mph (272 km/h).
Weights: Empty equipped, 2,535 lb (1 150 kg); max take-off, 4,751 lb (2 155 kg).
Armament: (Weapons training) Four wing hardpoints stressed for 441 lb (200 kg) inboard and 353 lb (160 kg) outboard.
Status: Turbo Orlik (modified from third prototype Orlik) flown on 13 July 1986, but destroyed in January 1987. A second prototype to complete certification scheduled to enter flight test during 1988.
Notes: Turbo Orlik developed as potential export version of the piston-engined Orlik (see 1986 edition) which is intended for service with the Polish Air Force. Development of the Turbo Orlik has been undertaken with the assistance of Airtech Canada. A noteworthy feature of the Turbo Orlik is its low aspect ratio wing permitting simulation of the roll yaw and sink rate characteristics of high-speed combat aircraft.

Dimensions: Span, 26 ft 3 in (8,00 m); length, 28 ft $5\frac{3}{4}$ in (8,68 m); height, 11 ft 7 in (3,53 m); wing area, 132·18 sq ft (12,28 m²).

ROCKWELL B-1B

Country of Origin: USA.

Type: Strategic bomber and cruise missile carrier.

Power Plant: Four 30,780 lb st (13 960 kgp) General Electric F101-GE-102 turbofans.

Performance: Max speed (without external load), 795 mph (1 280 km/h) or Mach = 1·25 above 36,000 ft (10 975 m); low-level penetration speed, 610 mph (980 km/h) or Mach = 0·8 at 200 ft (60 m); unrefuelled range (approx), 7,500 mls (12 070 km).

Weights: Empty, 184,300 lb (83 500 kg); empty equipped, 192,000 lb (87 090 kg); design flight, 395,000 lb (179 172 kg); max take-off, 477,000 lb (216 367 kg).

Accommodation: Flight crew of four comprising pilot, co-pilot/navigator, defensive systems operator and offensive systems operator.

Armament: Two fuselage weapons bays to carry up to 84 500-lb (227-kg) Mk 82 bombs, 24 2,000-lb (908-kg) Mk 84 bombs, 24 2,439-lb (1 106-kg) B-83 nuclear bombs, or eight AGM-86B cruise missiles plus 12 AGM-69 defence-suppression missiles. Up to 44 Mk 82 bombs or 14 720-lb (327-kg) B-61 nuclear bombs, or 14 AGM-86B missiles or eight hardpoints.

Status: First of 100 production B-1Bs flown on 18 October 1984, with initial deliveries commencing 29 June 1985. Initial operational capability was attained in October 1986, and 100th aircraft to be delivered April 1988.

Notes: An extensively revised derivative of the B-1A, the first of four prototypes of which flew on 23 December 1974, the B-1B is expected to operate primarily at high subsonic speeds at low altitudes. Apart from serving to launch cruise missiles or to deliver free-fall bombs, the B-1B can fulfil long-range sea surveillance, aerial mine-laying and other roles.

ROCKWELL B-1B

Dimensions: Span (15 deg sweep), 136 ft 8½ in (41,67 m), (67·5 deg sweep), 78 ft 2½ in (23,84 m); length, 147 ft 0 in (44,81 m); height, 34 ft 0 in (10,36 m); wing area (approx), 1,950 sq ft (181,20 m²).

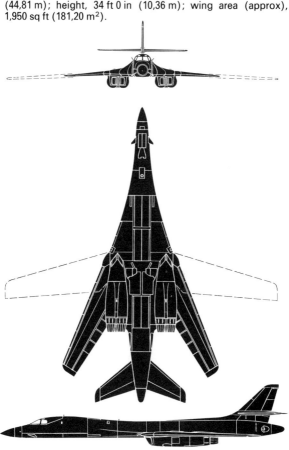

SAAB 39 GRIPEN

Country of Origin: Sweden.

Type: Single-seat multi-role fighter.

Power Plant: One 12,150 lb st (5 510 kgp) dry and 18,100 lb st (8 210 kgp) General Electric/Volvo RM 12 turbofan.

Performance: No details available for publication, but max speed is expected to range from 914 mph (1 470 km/h), or Mach = 1·2, at sea level to 1,450 mph (2 555 km/h), or Mach = 2·2, above 36,000 ft (10 975 m), tactical radius (intercept mission with two Rb 24 Sidewinder and two Rb 72 Sky Flash AAMs) exceeding 250 mls (400 km).

Weights: Approx clean loaded, 17,635 lb (8 000 kg).

Armament: One 27-mm Mauser BK 27 cannon and (intercept) four Rb 72 Sky Flash and two Rb 24 Sidewinder AAMs, or (attack mission) various electro-optically guided ASMs, area weapons or RBS 15F anti-shipping missiles on wing stations.

Status: First of five prototypes scheduled to enter flight test mid 1988. Initial contract for 30 aircraft with options on further 110 aircraft, and first deliveries anticipated 1992. Overall Swedish Air Force requirement exceeding 300 aircraft by 2010.

Notes: The Gripen (Griffon), or JAS 39, has been designed to fulfil fighter, attack and reconnaissance roles and will carry permanently all necessary hardware and software for all three tasks, mission changes calling only for provision of appropriate external stores. The Gripen makes extensive use of composites in its structure, has a triple-redundant digital fly-by-wire control system, all-moving canards and the ability to operate from 875 yard (800-m) airstrips. A two-seat conversion training version, the JAS 39B, was being proposed at the beginning of 1988.

SAAB 39 GRIPEN

Dimensions: (Approximate) Span, 26 ft 3 in (8,00 m); length, 46 ft 0 in (14,00 m).

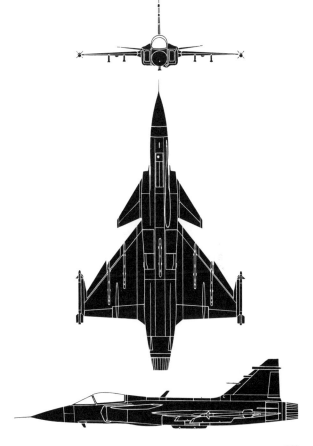

SAAB SF340

Country of Origin: Sweden.
Type: Regional commercial and corporate transport.
Power Plant: Two 1,735 shp General Electric CT7-5A2 turboprops.
Performance: Max cruising speed, 320 mph (515 km/h) at 15,000 ft (4 570 m); econ cruise, 300 mph (484 km/h) at 25,000 ft (7 620 m); max initial climb, 1,765 ft/min (8,94 m/sec); range (max payload), 904 mls (1 455 km), (max fuel), 2,470 mls (3 975 km).
Weights: Operational empty (typical), 17,215 lb (7 810 kg); max take-off, 27,275 lb (12 370 kg).
Accommodation: Flight crew of two and standard regional airline arrangement for 35 passengers three abreast. Various optional arrangements are available for the corporate transport version up to 16 passengers.
Status: First of three prototypes flown on 25 January 1983. First production aircraft flown on 5 March 1984. The 100th aircraft was accepted (by Salair) on 14 September 1987, and total orders were 132 of which 108 had been delivered by beginning of 1988 when production was three monthly.
Notes: SF340 originally developed jointly with Fairchild of the USA, latter relinquishing partnership on 1 November 1985, and the 109th aircraft is the first completely built by Saab-Scania. Consideration of stretched versions (40–50 seats) was continuing at the beginning of 1988, by which time an improved performance version, the SF340B with 1,870 shp CT7-9B engines, had been launched. To be certificated spring 1989, the SF340B has a longer-span tailplane, the same payload capacity, but increased operating weights and a max payload range of 921 mls (1 482 km).

SAAB SF340

Dimensions: Span, 70 ft 4 in (21,44 m); length, 64 ft 6 in (19,67 m); height, 22 ft 6 in (6,87 m); wing area, 450 sq ft (41,81 m²).

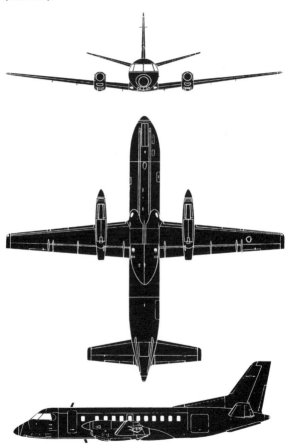

SHENYANG J-8B (F-8 II)

Country of Origin: China.
Type: Single-seat multi-role fighter.
Power Plant: Two 14,550 lb st (6 600 kgp) reheat Chengdu Wopen-13 turbojets.
Performance: Max speed, 1,452 mph (2 337 km/h) above 36,000 ft (10 975 m), or Mach=2·2; service ceiling, 65,620 ft (20 000 m); max range (with external tanks on fuselage centreline and outboard wing stations), 1,367 mls (2 200 km).
Weights: Empty, 21,649 lb (9 820 kg); normal loaded, 31,525 lb (14 300 kg); max take-off, 39,242 lb (17 800 kg).
Armament: Two 23-mm twin-barrel cannon and (intercept mission) up to six PL-2B or PL-7 infra-red or semi-active radar homing AAMs, or (close air support) up to 8,818 lb (4 000 kg) of ordnance distributed between one fuselage and six wing stores stations.
Status: The first prototype J-8B was flown mid-1985, and production aircraft are expected to be delivered to the People's Republic of China Air Force from 1988–89.
Notes: The J-8B (also referred to by the export designation of F-8 II) is a development of the early 'seventies J 8 which was manufactured in limited numbers (see 1986 edition). It differs from the earlier model fundamentally in replacing the circular pitot air intake with lateral intakes, the new nose section permitting installation of a dual-role radar. It also possesses uprated engines. During 1986, agreement was reached with the US Government for the supply of avionics system kits for installation in the J-8B, flight testing with the US equipment being expected to commence in 1991–92. At the beginning of 1988, consideration was being given to re-engining the J-8B with General Electric F404s.

SHENYANG J-8B (F-8 II)

Dimensions: Span, 30 ft $7\frac{7}{8}$ in (9,34 m); length, 70 ft 10 in (21,59 m) including probe; height, 17 ft 9 in (5,41 m); wing area, 454·25 sq ft (42,20 m^2).

SHORTS 360-300

Country of Origin: United Kingdom.
Type: Regional commercial transport.
Power Plant: Two 1,424 shp Pratt & Whitney Canada PT6A-67R turboprops.
Performance: Max cruising speed, 251 mph (404 km/h) at 10,000 ft (3 050 m); long range cruise, 207 mph (333 km/h) at 10,000 ft (3 050 m); range (with max payload), 259 mls (417 km), (max fuel), 992 mls (1 596 km).
Weights: Operational empty, 16,950 lb (7 688 kg); max take-off, 27,100 lb (12 292 kg).
Accommodation: Flight crew of two with all-passenger cabin arrangements for 36–39 seats three abreast, and optional 'combi' (one ton of cargo and 24 passengers or (360–300F) all-freight (10,000 lb/4 536 kg) arrangements.
Status: Prototype flown on 1 June 1981, with first production aircraft following on 19 August 1982 and entering service (with Suburban Airlines) in the following December. The Shorts 360-300 was introduced in 1987. Orders and options (all versions) totalled approximately 150 aircraft at the beginning of 1988, by which time 128 had been delivered.
Notes: The -300 version of the Shorts 360 has been upgraded with the use of -67R engines driving six-bladed propellers, cambered lift struts, refined engine nacelles and improved avionics. The basic Shorts 360 is a growth version of the Shorts 330 (see 1983 edition), which continues in production in parallel. The later aircraft differs from its progenitor primarily in having a 3-ft (91-cm) cabin stretch ahead of the wing and an entirely redesigned rear fuselage and tail assembly. The fuselage stretch has permitted the insertion of two–three additional three-seat rows in the main cabin and has resulted in reduced aerodynamic drag by comparison with the earlier aircraft.

SHORTS 360-300

Dimensions: Span, 74 ft 10 in (22,81 m); length, 70 ft 10 in (21,59 m); height, 23 ft 8 in (7,21 m); wing area, 454 sq ft (42,18 m²).

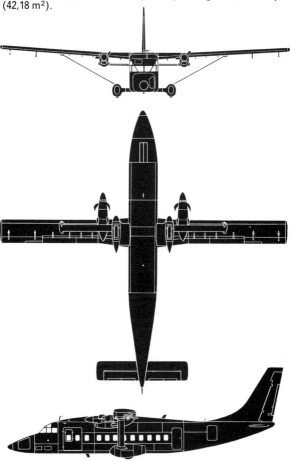

SHORTS S312 TUCANO

Country of Origin: United Kingdom (Brazil).
Type: Tandem two-seat basic trainer.
Power Plant: One 1,100 shp Garrett TPE331-12B/701A turboprop.
Performance: Max speed (at 4,850 lb/2 200 kg), 320 mph (515 km/h) at 14,000 ft (4,270 m), (at 5,732 lb/2 600 kg), 315 mph (508 km/h) at 12,500 ft (3 810 m); econ cruise, 253 mph (407 km/h) at 20,000 ft (6 100 m); max initial climb, 3,510 ft/min (17,83 m/sec); range (with 30 min reserves), 1,082 mls (1 742 km) at 25,000 ft (7 620 m), (with two 72·6 Imp gal/300 l external tanks), 2,073 mls (3 335 km).
Weights: Basic empty, 4,447 lb (2 017 kg); max take-off (aerobatic), 5,842 lb (2 650 kg), (weapons configuration), 7,220 lb (3 275 kg).
Armament: (Training and counter insurgency) Four wing stations for (typical) two 7,62-mm C-2 machine gun pods and two 250-lb (113,4-kg) bombs, paired 5-in (12,7-cm) rockets, or LM-37/7A or LM-70/7 rocket pods.
Status: Brazilian-built prototype flown on 14 February 1986, with first Shorts-built aircraft having flown 30 December 1986. Total of 130 ordered by the RAF, with service to commence during 1988. Production to attain four monthly in 1989.
Notes: The Shorts Tucano has been developed from the EMB-312 Tucano (see pages 96–7) specifically to meet RAF requirements, embodying a new Garrett engine, structural strengthening for increased manœuvre loads and fatigue life, a new cockpit layout, a ventral air brake, etc.

SHORTS S312 TUCANO

Dimensions: Span, 37 ft 0 in (11,28 m); length, 32 ft 4¼ in (9,86 m); height, 11 ft 1⅞ in (3,40 m); wing area, 208·07 sq ft (19,33 m²).

SIAI MARCHETTI S.211

Country of Origin: Italy.

Type: Tandem two-seat basic trainer.

Power Plant: One 2,500 lb st (1 134 kgp) Pratt & Whitney Canada JT15D-4C turbofan.

Performance: Max speed, 414 mph (667 km/h) at 20,000 ft (6 095 m), 371 mph (597 km/h) at sea level; max initial climb, 3,800 ft/min (19,30 m/sec); max range (internal fuel with 30 min reserves), 1,036 mls (1 668 km); ferry range (with two 77 Imp gal/350 l external tanks), 1,543 mls (2 483 km).

Weights: Empty equipped, 3,560 lb (1 615 kg); max take-off (clean), 5,952 lb (2 700 kg), (with external stores), 6,834 lb (3 100 kg).

Armament: (Training and light attack) Max external load of 1,320 lb (600 kg) distributed between four wing stations.

Status: First of three prototypes flown on 10 April 1981, and first production example (for Singapore) flown on 4 October 1984, with deliveries commencing in the following year. Thirty ordered by Singapore (of which 20 being supplied as partial kits) with deliveries continuing at beginning of 1988. Four ordered by Haiti.

Notes: Intended to compete realistically in operating cost with current turboprop-powered basic trainers, the S.211 can be used for a proportion of the primary instructional phase. It possesses the lowest airframe weight of any current pure jet trainer other than the Jet Squalus (see pages 174–5), and versions with more advanced avionics and an uprated engine are being offered. These, equipped with an advanced lightweight head-up display and navigation computer, combine enhanced training capability with the light strike task. At the beginning of 1988, a lengthened version was being studied in collaboration with Singapore Aircraft Industries.

SIAI MARCHETTI S.211

Dimensions: Span, 27 ft 8 in (8,43 m); length, 30 ft 6½ in (9,31 m); height, 12 ft 5½ in (3,80 m); wing area, 135·63 sq ft (12,60 m²).

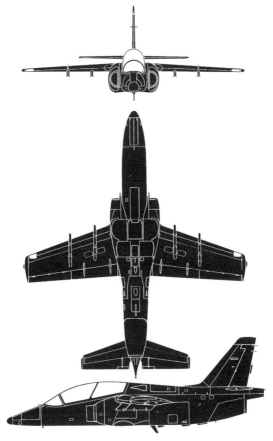

SOCATA/MOONEY TBM 700

Country of Origin: France and USA.
Type: Light business executive transport.
Power Plant: One 700 shp Pratt & Whitney Canada PT6A-40/1 turboprop.
Performance: (Estimated) Max cruising speed, 345 mph (556 km/h) at 25,000 ft (7 620 m); max initial climb, 2,300 ft/min (11,7 m/sec); range (45 min reserves), 1,785 mls (2 870 km) at max cruise and 2,300 mls (3 705 km) at 288 mph (463 km/h) with three occupants, 1,325 mls (2 130 km) at max cruise and 1,610 mls (2 590 km) at 288 mph (463 km/h) with six occupants.
Weights: Empty, 3,290 lb (1 492 kg); max take-off, 5,890 lb (2 672 kg).
Accommodation: Two pilots side by side and up to six passengers in main cabin. Four-passenger arrangement with club seating and central aisle.
Status: Prototype TBM 700 scheduled to commence flight test during summer of 1988, with certification planned for 1989 and initial deliveries to commence at end of that year.
Notes: The TBM 700 is a joint venture between the SOCATA subsidiary of Aérospatial (France) and Mooney Aircraft (USA), and final assembly lines are to be established in both countries. The TBM 700 takes advantage of flight test results obtained with the pressurised Mooney M301 and uses basically the same airframe, SOCATA refinements being primarily concerned with the wing. One third of the development cost of the TBM 700 is being funded by a French governmental loan, and orders for the first two production aircraft were announced in June 1987.

SOCATA/MOONEY TBM 700

Dimensions: Span, 39 ft 10¾ in (12,16 m); length, 34 ft 2½ in (10,43 m); height, 13 ft 1 in (3,99 m).

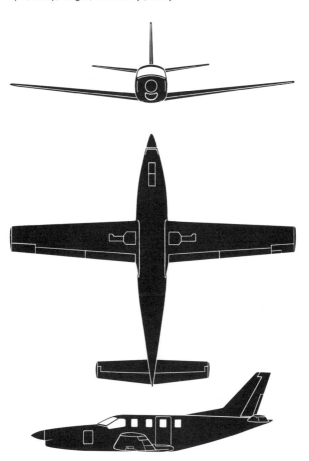

SUKHOI SU-24 (FENCER)

Country of Origin: USSR.

Type: Deep penetration interdictor and strike aircraft.

Power Plant: Two 17,675 lb st (8 020 kgp) dry and 25,350 lb st (11 500 kgp) reheat Tumansky R-29B turbojets.

Performance: (Estimated) Max sustained speed (without external stores, 1,440 mph (2 317 km/h), or Mach = 2·18, above 36,000 ft (11 000 m), 915 mph (1 470 km/h), or Mach = 1·2, at sea level; tactical radius (with 6,615-lb/3 000-kg warload and two 660 Imp gal/3 000 l drop tanks), 930 mls (1 500 km) with HI-LO-LO-HI mission profile.

Weights: (Estimated) Empty equipped, 41,890 lb (19 000 kg); max take-off, 85,000–90,000 lb (38 560–40 800 kg).

Armament: One six-barrel 30-mm rotary cannon and up to (approx) 13,230 lb (6 000 kg) of ordnance on four fuselage and four wing hardpoints, including AS-10 *Karen*, AS-11, AS-12 *Kegler*, AS-13 and AS-14 *Kedge* air-to-surface missiles.

Status: Prototypes believed first flown 1969–70, with initial operational status from late 1974. Some 850 reportedly in SovAF service (in both strike and recce roles) at beginning of 1988, plus some 60 with SovNavAir.

Notes: Several versions of the Su-24 have been deployed by the SovAF, that illustrated and referred to by NATO as *Fencer-D* having been introduced in 1983. This version introduced flight refuelling capability, additional fin area and enlarged glove pylons. Like the preceding *Fencer-C*, the *-D* replaced the Lyulka AL-21F engines of the original production series with R-29B units. The *Fencer-E* is a recce version operated by the Soviet Navy. The Su-24 has four sweep angle settings (16, 45, 55 and 68 deg) and is crewed by pilot and weapon systems operator side by side.

SUKHOI SU-24 (FENCER)

Dimensions: (Estimated) Span (16 deg sweep), 56 ft 6 in (17,25 m), (68 deg sweep), 33 ft 9 in (10,30 m); length (excluding probe), 72 ft 2 in (22,00 m); height, 18 ft 0 in (5,50 m).

SUKHOI SU-25 (FROGFOOT)

Country of Origin: USSR.
Type: Single-seat attack and close air support aircraft.
Power Plant: Two 11,240 lb st (5 100 kgp) Tumansky R-13-300 turbojets.
Performance: (Estimated) Max speed (without external stores), 545 mph (877 km/h) at 10,000 ft (3 050 m) or Mach = 0·757; combat radius (with 8,820 lb/4 000 kg of ordnance and allowance for 30 min loiter at 5,000 ft/1 525 m), 340 mls (546 km) HI-LO-LO-HI; ferry range (with four 108 Imp gal/490 l external tanks), 1,800 mls (2 895 km).
Weights: Empty, 20,950 lb (9 500 kg); max take-off, 41,890–44,090 lb (19 000–20 000 kg).
Armament: One 30-mm cannon and up to 8,820 lb (4 000 kg) of ordnance on 10 wing hardpoints, including 57-mm and 80-mm unguided rockets, 1,100-lb (500-kg) retarded cluster bombs, etc. Air-to-air missiles for self defence may be carried on outboard hardpoints.
Status: The Su-25 was first observed under test in the late 'seventies, prototypes having presumably flown during 1977–78, with initial deliveries to the Soviet Air Forces following in 1980–81. The first export customer for the Su-25 was Czechoslovakia, and production was continuing at the beginning of 1988 at Tbilisi at a rate of 100 aircraft annually.
Notes: The Su-25 is broadly comparable with the USAF's Fairchild A-10A Thunderbolt II. It features a levered-suspension type undercarriage with low-pressure tyres suitable for rough field operation and wingtip fairings of flattened ovoid section which incorporate split spoilers operated symmetrically or differentially to aid low-altitude manœuvrability. Operators of the Su-25 include Hungary and Iraq.

SUKHOI SU-25 (FROGFOOT)

Dimensions: (Estimated) Span, 46 ft 7 in (14,20 m); length (including nose probes), 49 ft 10½ in (15,20 m); height, 15 ft 8 9/10 in (4,80 m). Wing area, 404·74 sq ft (37,60 m²).

SUKHOI SU-27 (FLANKER-B)

Country of Origin: USSR.

Type: Single-seat counterair fighter.

Power Plant: Two (probably) 20,000 lb st (9 070 kgp) dry and 30,000 lb st (13 610 kgp) reheat Tumansky R-32 turbofans.

Performance: (Estimated) Max speed, 1,320 mph (2 120 km/h), or Mach = 2·0, at altitude, 835 mph (1 345 km/h), or Mach = 1·1, at sea level; tactical radius (subsonic intercept mission with external fuel and six AAMs), 930 mls (1 500 km).

Weights: (Estimated) Normal loaded (air–air mission), 45,000 lb (20 400 kg); max take-off, 63,500 lb (28 800 kg).

Armament: One 30-mm six-barrel rotary cannon in starboard fuselage side and up to 10 air-to-air missiles usually comprising six AA-10 Alamo medium-range missiles (two beneath fuselage and between engine air intake ducts, two beneath the ducts and two on inboard wing pylons) and four AA-11 Archer short-range missiles (two on outer wing pylons and two at wingtips).

Status: First deployed to Kola Peninsula in 1986, the Su-27 is believed to have entered flight test (Flanker-A) in 1977. It is currently in series production at Komsomolsk, with some 100 in service by the beginning of 1988.

Notes: Comparable with the F-15 Eagle and possessing track-while-scan radar, a pulse-Doppler lookdown/shootdown weapon system, infrared search and tracking, and a digital data link, the Su-27 is believed to be the aircraft (referred to as the P-42) that established several time-to-altitude records in November–December 1986. These included 25·4 seconds to 9,840 ft (3 000 m), 37·1 seconds to 19·685 ft (6 000 m), 47·1 seconds to 29,530 ft (9 000 m) and 58·14 seconds to 39,370 ft (12 000 m).

SUKHOI SU-27 (FLANKER-B)

Dimensions: (Estimated) Span, 48 ft 3 in (14,70 m); length (excluding probe), 70 ft 10 in (21,60 m); height, 18 ft 0 in (5,50 m); wing area, 550 sq ft (51,00 m²).

TUPOLEV TU-26 (BACKFIRE-C)

Country of Origin: USSR.
Type: Medium-range strategic bomber and maritime strike/reconnaissance aircraft.
Power Plant: Two (estimated) 33,070 lb st (15 000 kgp) dry and 46,300 lb st (21 000 kgp) reheat Kuznetsov turbofans.
Performance: (Estimated) Max speed (short-period dash), 1,265 mph (2 036 km/h), or Mach = 1·91, at 39,370 ft (12 000 m), (sustained), 1,056 mph (1 700 km/h), or Mach = 1·6, 685 mph (1 100 km/h), or Mach = 0·9, at sea level; combat radius (unrefuelled high-altitude subsonic mission profile with single AS-4 ASM), 2,160 mls (4 200 km).
Weights: (Estimated) Max take-off, 285,000 lb (129 275 kg).
Armament: Remotely-controlled tail barbette with twin 23-mm cannon. Internal load of free-falling weapons up to 12,345 lb (5 600 kg), one AS-4 Kitchen inertially-guided stand-off missile semi-recessed on fuselage centreline, or two AS-4s suspended from fixed wing centre section.
Status: Backfire-C is latest known service version of the Tu-26 (alias Tu-22M) of which some 400–420 (all versions) in service at beginning of 1988.
Notes: Backfire-C features new air intake geometry.

TUPOLEV TU-26 (BACKFIRE-C)

Dimensions: (Estimated) Span (20 deg sweep), 112 ft 0 in
(34,14 m), (55 deg sweep), 86 ft 0 in (26,20 m); length, 130 ft
0 in (39,62 m); wing area, 1,800 sq ft (167,22 m²).

TUPOLEV (BLACKJACK-A)

Country of Origin: USSR.

Type: Long-range strategic bomber and maritime strike/reconnaissance aircraft.

Power Plant: Four (approx) 30,000 lb st (13 610 kgp) dry and 50,000 lb st (22 680 kgp) reheat turbofans.

Performance: (Estimated) Max (over-target dash) speed, 1,380 mph (2 220 km/h) at 40,000 ft (12 200 m), or Mach = 2·09; range cruise, 595 mph (960 km/h) at 45,000 ft (13 720 m), or Mach = 0·9; unrefuelled combat radius (subsonic cruise, supersonic high-altitude dash and transonic low-altitude penetration) 4,540 mls (7 300 km).

Weights: (Estimated) Empty, 260,000 lb (117 950 kg); max take-off, 590,000 lb (267 625 kg).

Armament: Primary weapons are expected to be 1,850-mile (3 000-km) range AS-15 Kent subsonic low-altitude cruise missile and the supersonic BL-10 missile, but provision will be made for free-falling bombs or mix of missiles and bombs up to an estimated maximum of 36,000 lb (16 330 kg).

Status: First seen under test (at Ramenskoye, near Moscow) in 1979, the Blackjack apparently entered production at Kazan in 1984–85, and initial operational capability is anticipated in 1988, by the beginning of which some seven–eight were flying, according to Pentagon sources.

Notes: Blackjack is expected to initially replace the Bear-A in the Soviet strategic bombing force, supplementing Bear-H. Some 25 per cent larger than the Rockwell B-1B, Blackjack was initially known by the provisional reporting designation of Ram-P (indicating that it had first been seen at Ramenskoye). It is anticipated that a series of about 100 bombers of this type will be built at a massive new complex that has been constructed at Kazan.

TUPOLEV (BLACKJACK-A)

Dimensions: (Estimated) Span (minimum sweep), 150 ft 0 in (54,00 m), (maximum sweep), 101 ft 0 in (30,75 m); length, 175 ft 0 in (53,35 m); wing area, 2,500 sq ft (232,25 m²).

TUPOLEV TU-204

Country of Origin: USSR.

Type: Medium-haul commercial airliner.

Power Plant: Two 35,280 lb st (16 000 kgp) Soloviev D-90A turbofans.

Performance: (Estimated) Max cruise speed, 528 mph (850 km/h) at 39,375 ft (12 000 m); econ cruise, 503 mph (810 km/h) at 36,100 ft (11 000 m); max cruise altitude, 40,025 ft (11 000 m); range (with 46,296-lb/21 000-kg payload), 1,490 mls (2 400 km), (with 34,390-lb/15 600-kg payload), 2,485 mls (4 000 km).

Weights: Empty equipped, 124,780 lb (56 600 kg); max take-off, 207,230 lb (94 000 kg).

Accommodation: Flight crew of two (with option of three) and up to 214 passengers six abreast with central aisle and typical mixed-class arrangement for 12 first class, 47 business class and 111 tourist class passengers.

Status: First Tu-204 scheduled to enter flight test in first half of 1988, with initial production deliveries (to Aeroflot) commencing 1990–91.

Notes: A narrow-body medium-haul transport in the same general category as the Boeing 757, the Tu-204 makes extensive use of new materials, including composites, to achieve a low specific structure weight. The structure has been designed for a service life of 45,000 hours and 30,000 landings, and advanced systems are employed, these apparently including 'fly-by-wire'. The cockpit has six full-colour EFIS displays and the Tu-204 has triple inertial navigation systems. The Tu-204 is one of a trio of new airliners (the others being the Il-96-300 and the Il-114) designed to re-equip Aeroflot from the early 'nineties, and is intended to succeed such types as the Tu-154M (see 1987 edition).

TUPOLEV TU-204

Dimensions: Span, 137 ft 9½ in (42,00 m); length, 147 ft 7½ in (45,00 m).

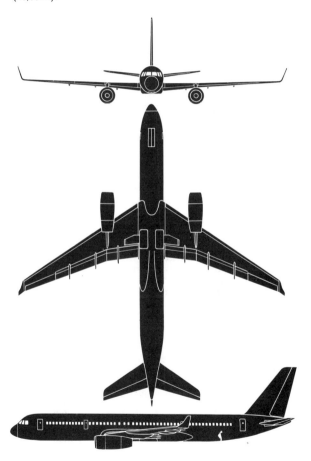

UTVA LASTA

Country of Origin: Yugoslavia.

Type: Tandem two-seat primary/basic trainer.

Power Plant: One 300 hp Textron Lycoming AEIO-540-L1B5-D six-cylinder horizontally-opposed engine.

Performance: Max speed, 214 mph (345 km/h) at sea level; max initial climb (at 3,593 lb/1 630 kg), 1,772 ft/min (9,0 m/sec).

Weights: Empty equipped, 2,337 lb (1 060 kg); max take-off, 3,593 lb (1 630 kg).

Armament: (Weapons training) Two universal ordnance pods with a total weight of 529 lb (240 kg), two 16-tube 57-mm rocket pods or two twin 7,62-mm machine gun pods.

Status: First of two prototypes flown for the first time during summer of 1985, with pre-series of 10 delivered for service evaluation 1987, and reported Yugoslav Air Force requirement for 60–70 aircraft.

Notes: Designed by the Air Force Technical Institute at Žarkovo and now being manufactured by the UTVA concern at Pančevo, the Lasta (Swallow) is scheduled to succeed the UTVA 75 in the flying training syllabus of both para-military and military schools. The cockpits of the Lasta are based on those of the Soko Galeb 4 (see 1986 edition) in which Yugoslav Air Force students graduate for advanced flying training. During 1987, an initial course graduated on the pre-series Lasta before progressing to the Galeb 4 to establish the future training curriculum. The Galeb is in the same category as the TB 30 Epsilon and T-35 Pillán (which see), and consideration is reportedly being given to the development of a version powered by a turboprop.

UTVA LASTA

Dimensions: Span, 27 ft 4⅓ in (8,34 m); length, 26 ft 4½ in (8,04 m); height, 14 ft 7¼ in (4,45 m); wing area, 118·4 sq ft (11,00 m²).

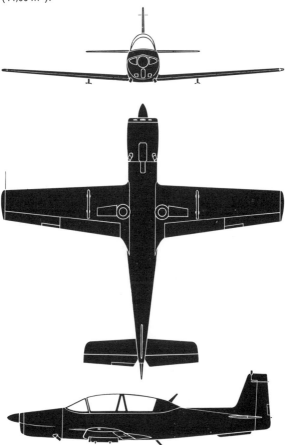

VALMET L-90 TP REDIGO

Country of Origin: Finland.

Type: Side-by-side two-seat primary/basic trainer.

Power Plant: One 420 shp (flat-rated to 360 shp) Allison 250-B17D or 450 shp Turboméca TM.319 turboprop.

Performance: (Allison 250 at 2,976 lb/1 350 kg) Max speed, 208 mph (335 km/h) at 5,000 ft (1 525 m); cruise (75% power), 190 mph (305 km/h) at 9,840 ft (3 000 m); max initial climb, 1,930 ft/min (9,80 m/sec); time to 16,405 ft (5 000 m), 11·5 min; max range, 1,070 mls (1 725 km); endurance, 5·0 hrs.

Weights: Basic empty, 1,960 lb (889 kg); max take-off (aerobatic), 2,980 lb (1 352 kg), (normal), 3,530 lb (1 601 kg), (utility with external load), 4,190 lb (1 900 kg).

Armament: (Weapons training and light strike) Max external load of 1,764 lb (800 kg) distributed between six wing stations, typical loads (when flown as single-seater) including four 330·5-lb (150-kg) bombs or two 551-lb (250-kg) bombs plus two flare pods.

Status: The Allison-powered first prototype Redigo was flown in July 1986, and the second, Turboméca-powered prototype was flown on 3 December 1987.

Notes: A derivative of the L-80 TP (see 1986 edition), which flew as a prototype on 12 February 1985, and, utilising the basic fuselage of the earlier piston-engined L-70, the Redigo is one of the lightest of the current generation of turboprop-powered instructional aircraft and is expected to gain certification mid-1988. The Redigo is being offered to potential customers with either Allison or Turboméca engine and will be available for delivery from 1989–90. The Redigo is fully aerobatic and stressed for +7*g* and −3·5*g*, the Turboméca-powered version offering a slightly superior climb rate and level speed.

VALMET L-90 TP REDIGO

Dimensions: Span, 33 ft 11 in (10,34 m); length, 25 ft 11 in (7,90 m); height, 9 ft 4¼ in (2,85 m); wing area, 158·77 sq ft (14,75 m²).

XAC Y-7-100

Country of Origin: China (USSR).
Type: Regional commercial transport.
Power Plant: Two 2,790 shp Shanghai WJ-5A-1 turboprops.
Performance: Max speed, 322 mph (518 km/h); max cruise, 301 mph (484 km/h) at 13,125 ft (4 000 m); econ cruise, 263 mph (423 km/h) at 19,685 ft (6 000 m); max initial climb, 1,504 ft/min (7,64 m/sec); service ceiling, 28,700 ft (8 750 m); range (with 52 passengers), 565 mls (910 km), (max standard fuel), 1,180 mls (1 900 km), (with auxiliary tank), 1,504 mls (2 420 km).
Weights: Operational empty, 32,849 lb (14 900 kg); max take-off, 48,060 lb (21 800 kg).
Accommodation: Flight crew of three and standard arrangement for 52 passengers four abreast with central aisle.
Status: An upgraded version of the Y-7, a reverse-engineered derivative of the Antonov An-24, the Y-7-100 was in production at Xian at the beginning of 1988 against an initial order placed by the Civil Aviation Administration of China for 40 aircraft, deliveries of which commenced late 1986.
Notes: The Xian Aircraft Company (XAC) built three flight test Y-7s, certification being obtained in 1980, subsequently building 24 series aircraft for the CAAC before introducing the Y-7-100. The latter has a re-engineered cockpit, western avionics, reconfigured interior, and, on later examples, winglets (as illustrated on opposite page). The Y-7-200, scheduled to become available late in 1988, will afford improved fuel consumption, and the Y-7-300 will introduce the use of composites to save weight and will feature a redesigned undercarriage.

Dimensions: Span, 97 ft 2¾ in (29,64 m); length, 77 ft 9½ in (23,71 m); height, 28 ft 0¾ in (8,55 m); wing area, 807·1 sq ft (74,98 m²).

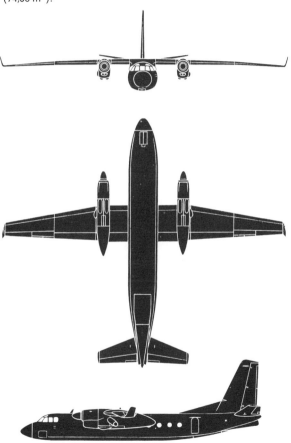

YAKOVLEV YAK-38 (FORGER-A)

Country of Origin: USSR.
Type: Single-seat shipboard air defence and strike fighter.
Power Plant: One 17,985 lb st (8 160 kgp) Lyulka AL-21 lift/
cruise turbojet and two tandem-mounted 7,875 lb st (3 570 kgp)
Koliesov lift turbojets.
Performance: (Estimated) Max speed, 648 mph (1 042 km/h)
or Mach=0·85 at sea level, 627 mph (1 010 km/h) or Mach=
0·95 above 36,000 ft (10 970 m); max initial climb, 14,750 ft/min
(74,93 m/sec); service ceiling, 39,375 ft (12 000 m); combat
radius with max ordnance, 150 mls (240 km) LO-LO-LO, 230 mls
(370 km) HI-LO-HI, (air defence with two GSh-23 gun pods and
two drop tanks), 115 mls (185 km) with 1 hr 15 min on station.
Weights: (Estimated) Empty equipped 16,500 lb (7 485 kg);
max take-off, 25,794 lb (11 700 kg).
Armament: (Air Defence) Two AA-8 Aphid AAMs or two
podded 23-mm twin-barrel GSh-23 cannon, or (strike) up to
7,936 lb (3 600 kg) of bombs, air-to-surface missiles such as
AS-7 Kerry and drop tanks.
Status: Believed to have flown as a prototype in 1971, and
initially referred to as the Yak-36MP, the Yak-38 is deployed
aboard the carriers *Kiev*, *Minsk*, *Novorossisk* and *Kharkov*, each
vessel having a complement of 12 fighters of this type.
Notes: The Yak-38 is capable of rolling vertical take-offs as
distinct from orthodox short take-offs which benefit from wing-
induced lift, such RVTOs not usually exceeding 35 mph (56 km/
h). Primary operational tasks are fleet air defence against
shadowing maritime surveillance aircraft, reconnaissance and
anti-ship strike. The tandem two-seat instructional version is
referred to as Forger-B.

YAKOVLEV YAK-38 (FORGER-A)

Dimensions: (Estimated) Span, 24 ft 7 in (7,50 m); length, 52 ft 6 in (16,00 m); height, 11 ft 0 in (3,35 m); wing area, 199·14 sq ft (18,50 m^2).

YAKOVLEV YAK-42 (CLOBBER)

Country of Origin: USSR.

Type: Medium-range commercial transport.

Power Plant: Three 14,330 lb st (6 500 kgp) Lotarev D-36 turbofans.

Performance: Max cruising speed, 503 mph (810 km/h) at 25,000 ft (7 620 m); econ cruise, 466 mph (750 km/h) at 25,000 ft (7 620 m); range (with max payload), 559 mls (900 km), (with 23,150-lb/10 500-kg payload), 1,242 mls (2 000 km), (with 14,330-lb/6 500-kg payload), 1,864 mls (3 000 km).

Weights: Empty, 63,845 lb (28 960 kg); max take-off, 117,950 lb (53 500 kg).

Accommodation: Crew of two on flight deck and single-class cabin with 120 seats six abreast with central aisle.

Status: First of three prototypes flown on 7 March 1975, and production of initial series of 200 initiated at Smolensk in 1978, with 10 flown by mid-1981. Withdrawn from service for unspecified reason in 1982, but restored to Aeroflot routes in 1984, when production was resumed.

Notes: At the beginning of 1988, development was in process of a 'stretched' version of the basic design designated Yak-42M. This features a 14 ft 9 in (4,50 m) longer fuselage to accommodate 156–168 passengers, max take-off weight being increased to 145,000 lb (66 000 kg). The engines of the Yak-42M are 16,550 lb st (7 500 kgp) Lotarev D-436 turbofans and payload over a 1,550-mile (2 500-km) range is claimed to be 35,275 lb (16 000 kg). The Yak-42 programme has suffered a number of delays resulting from unspecified causes, but production for Aeroflot is now continuing at Smolensk of both the basic Yak-42 and the stretched Yak-42M, the latter being scheduled to enter service during the course of 1988.

YAKOVLEV YAK-42 (CLOBBER)

Dimensions: Span, 114 ft 5¼ in (34,88 m); length, 119 ft 4¼ in (36,38 m); height, 32 ft 1¾ in (9,80 m); wing area, 1,615 sq ft (150,00 m²).

AEROSPATIALE AS 332M1 SUPER PUMA

Country of Origin: France.
Type: Medium tactical transport helicopter.
Power Plant: Two 1,877 shp Turboméca Makila 1A1 turbo-shafts.
Performance: (At 19,840 lb/9 000 kg) Max speed, 173 mph (278 km/h); max cruise, 163 mph (262 km/h) at sea level; max inclined climb, 1,397 ft/min (7,1 m/sec); hovering ceiling (in ground effect), 8,856 ft (2 700 m); (out of ground effect), 5,248 ft (1 600 m); range, 523 mls (842 km).
Weights: Empty, 9,745 lb (4 420 kg); max take-off, 19,840 lb (9 000 kg), (with external load), 20,615 lb (9 350 kg).
Dimensions: Rotor diam, 51 ft 9¾ in (15,60 m); fuselage length, 48 ft 7¾ in (14,82 m).
Notes: The stretched version of the AS 332 was first flown on 10 October 1980, uprated versions of the military (AS 332M1) and civil (AS-332L1) versions having been introduced in 1986. More than 230 Super Pumas had been delivered by the end of 1987 when orders totalled in excess of 270. The AS 332F is a navalised ASW version with an overall length of 42 ft 1½ in (12,83 m) with rotor blades folded. Licence manufacture of the Super Puma is being undertaken in Indonesia as the NAS-332, and production by the parent company was continuing at a rate of two–three monthly at the beginning of 1988. The AS 332L can accommodate up to 22 passengers and the AS 332M can carry 25 troops and can be armed with 20-mm cannon or rocket launchers.

AEROSPATIALE AS 350L1 ECUREUIL

Country of Origin: France.

Type: Military six-seat general-purpose helicopter.

Power Plant: One 693 shp Turboméca Arriel 1 D turboshaft.

Performance: (At 4,850 lb/2 200 kg) Max speed, 169 mph (272 km/h); max cruise, 149 mph (240 km/h); normal cruise, 137 mph (220 km/h); max inclined climb, 1,500 ft/min (7,5 m/sec); hovering ceiling (in ground effect), 9,400 ft (2 870 m), (out of ground effect), 6,300 ft (1 920 m); range, 407 mls (655 km).

Weights: Empty, 2,575 lb (1 168 kg); max take-off, 4,850 lb (2 200 kg), (with external load), 5,400 lb (2 450 kg).

Dimensions: Rotor diam, 35 ft 0¾ in (10,69 m); fuselage length (tail rotor included), 35 ft 10⅓ in (10,93 m).

Notes: The AS 350L1 is the current military version of the single-engined Ecureuil (Squirrel). The Ecureuil was first flown on 27 June 1974 with a 615 shp Avco Lycoming LTS 101-600A2 turboshaft with which it is marketed in the USA as the AStar, the first Arriel-powered helicopter flying on 14 February 1975. The first AS 350L1 was flown in March 1985 with initial deliveries commencing in March 1986, and offers improved hot-and-high performance and an increased useful load. More than 1,050 single-engined Ecureuils (and AStars) had been delivered by the beginning of 1988, when production of both single- and twin-engined models (see page 222) was continuing at a rate of eight monthly. The AStar version is assembled and finished by Aérospatiale in Alberta.

AEROSPATIALE AS 355F2 ECUREUIL 2

Country of Origin: France.
Type: Six-seat light general-purpose utility helicopter.
Power Plant: Two 420 shp Allison 250-C20F turboshafts.
Performance: (At 5,600 lb/2 540 kg) Max speed, 169 mph (272 km/h); normal cruise, 139 mph (224 km/h); max inclined climb, 1,300 ft/min (6,5 m/sec); hovering ceiling (in ground effect), 5,900 ft (1 800 m), (out of ground effect), 4,430 ft (1 350 m); range, 438 mls (705 km).
Weights: Empty, 2,877 lb (1 305 kg); max take-off, 5,600 lb (2 540 kg), (with external load), 5,732 lb (2 600 kg).
Dimensions: Rotor diam, 35 ft 0¾ in (10,69 m); fuselage length (tail rotor included), 35 ft 10⅓ in (10,93 m).
Notes: Flown for the first time on 27 September 1979, the Ecureuil 2 employs an essentially similar airframe and similar dynamic components to those of the single-engined AS 350 Ecureuil (see page 221). From 1986, the production models have been the AS 355F2 (civil) and AS 355M2 (military) offering increased maximum take-off weights by comparison with preceding production models. The AS 355M2 can be armed with a 20-mm cannon and rocket launchers for the fire support role. By the beginning of 1988 some 380 Ecureuil 2 and TwinStar (the latter being the name applied for the North American market) helicopters had been ordered. The AS 355M has been ordered by the *Armée de l'Air* and the French Army, and may be fitted with a TOW installation. Some 200 TwinStars sold in North America.

AEROSPATIALE SA 365 DAUPHIN 2

Country of Origin: France.
Type: Multi-purpose and transport helicopter.
Power Plant: Two 700 shp Turboméca Arriel 1C turboshafts.
Performance: (SA 365N) Max speed, 190 mph (305 km/h); max continuous cruise, 173 mph (278 km/h) at sea level; max inclined climb, 1,279 ft/min (6,5 m/sec); hovering ceiling (in ground effect), 3,296 ft (1 005 m), (out of ground effect), 3,116 ft (950 m); range, 548 mls (882 km) at sea-level.
Weights: Empty, 4,511 lb (2 047 kg); max take-off, 8,818 lb (4 000 kg).
Dimensions: Rotor diam, 39 ft 1½ in (11,93 m); fuselage length (including tail rotor), 37 ft 6⅓ in (11,44 m).
Notes: Flown as a prototype on 31 March 1979, the SA 365 is the latest derivative of the basic Dauphin (see 1982 edition), and is being manufactured in four versions, the 10–14-seat commercial SA 365N, the military SA 365M Panther (see page 224), the navalised SA 365F with folding rotor, Agrion radar and four AS 15TT anti-ship missiles (20 ordered by Saudi Arabia for delivery from 1984) and the SA 366G, an Avco Lycoming LTS 101-750-powered search and rescue version for the US Coast Guard as the HH-65A Seaguard. Ninety of the last version have been procured by the US Coast Guard, with completion in 1985. Production of the SA 365N was five monthly at the beginning of 1988 when 400 had been delivered against total orders for some 420 Dauphin helicopters (all versions) for some 70 customers in 38 countries.

AEROSPATIALE SA 365M PANTHER

Country of Origin: France.
Type: Multi-role tactical helicopter.
Power Plant: Two 912 shp Turboméca TM 333-1M turbo-shafts.
Performance: (At 9,039 lb/4 100 kg) Max speed, 184 mph (296 km/h); max cruise, 170 mph (274 km/h) at sea level; max inclined climb, 1,575 ft/min (8 m/sec); hovering ceiling (in ground effect), 10,500 ft (3 200 m), (out of ground effect), 8,200 ft (2 500 m); range, 485 mls (780 km).
Weights: Empty, 5,070 lb (2 300 kg); max take-off, 9,039 lb (4 100 g).
Dimensions: Rotor diam, 39 ft 1½ in (11,93 m); fuselage length (including tail rotor), 39 ft 7 in (12,07 m).
Notes: A military derivative of the Dauphin 2 (see page 223), the first prototype of the SA 365M Panther was flown on 29 February 1984, with the first of two additional prototypes flying in April 1987. The Panther is intended for armed and light tactical transport missions. In the armed role it will use a Viviane roof-mounted day/night sight and weapon options include 20-mm Giat cannon in pods, pods of 22 68-mm rockets, eight Matra Mistral air–air missiles for anti-helicopter operations, or eight Hot anti-armour missiles. As an assault transport the Panther will accommodate 8–10 commandos, and provision is made for armour-plated seats, the armour protection of vital parts and jet diluters. The basic model has crash-worthy tanks and an instrument panel with CRT display.

AGUSTA A 109A MK II

Country of Origin: Italy.

Type: Eight-seat light utility helicopter.

Power Plant: Two 420 shp Allison 250-C20B turboshafts.

Performance: (At 5,402 lb/2 450 kg) Max speed, 193 mph (311 km/h); max continuous cruise, 173 mph (278 km/h); range cruise, 143 mph (231 km/h); max inclined climb rate, 1,820 ft/ min (9,25 m/sec); hovering ceiling (in ground effect), 9,800 ft (2 987 m); (out of ground effect), 6,800 ft (2 073 m); max range, 356 mls (573 km).

Weights: Empty equipped, 3,125 lb (1 418 kg); max take-off, 5,730 lb (2 600 kg).

Dimensions: Rotor diam, 36 ft 1 in (11,00 m); fuselage length, 35 ft 2½ in (10,73 m).

Notes: The A 109A Mk II is an improved model of the basic A 109A, the first of four prototypes of which flew on 4 August 1971, with customer deliveries commencing late 1976. Some 160 A 109A Mk IIs had been ordered by the beginning of 1988. The Mk II, which supplanted the initial model in production during 1981, has been the subject of numerous detail improvements, the transmission rating of the combined engines being increased from 692 to 740 shp, and the maximum continuous rating of each engine from 385 to 420 shp. An anti-armour version has been procured by Argentina, Libyan and Yugoslav forces. In 1984, a 'widebody' version of the A 109 Mk II was introduced. Flown in September of that year, this has new side panels adding 8 in (20 cm) to the cabin width.

AGUSTA A 129 MANGUSTA

Country of Origin: Italy.
Type: Two-seat light attack helicopter.
Power Plant: Two 1,050 shp Rolls-Royce Gem 2 Mk 1004D turboshafts.
Performance: (Estimated) Max speed, 173 mph (278 km/h); cruise (TOW configuration at 8,377 lb/3 800 kg), 149 mph (240 km/h) at 5,740 ft (1 750 m); max inclined climb (at 8,377 lb/ 3 800 kg), 2,087 ft/min (10,6 m/sec); hovering ceiling at 8,090 lb/3 670 kg), (in ground effect), 10,795 ft (3 290 m), (out of ground effect), 7,840 ft (2 390 m).
Weights: Mission, 8,080 lb (3 665 kg); max take-off, 8,377 lb (3 800 kg).
Dimensions: Rotor diam, 39 ft 0½ in (11,90 m); fuselage length, 39 ft 10 in (12,14 m).
Notes: The A 129 Mangusta (Mongoose) dedicated attack and anti-armour helicopter with full night/bad weather combat capability has been developed to an Italian Army requirement. The first of five flying prototypes commenced flight test on 15 September 1983, and first deliveries are scheduled for 1988, with 60 expected to be funded for the Italian Army and 20 considered during 1987 for the Netherlands Army. In typical anti-armour configuration, the A 129 will be armed with eight TOW missiles to which can be added 2·75-in (7-cm) rocket launchers for suppressive fire. The fourth prototype, flown in March 1985, has a unified electronic control system, combining flight controls, and weapon aiming and firing systems.

BELL AH-1S HUEYCOBRA

Country of Origin: USA.
Type: Two-seat light attack helicopter.
Power Plant: One 1,800 shp Avco Lycoming T53-L-703 turboshaft.
Performance: Max speed, 172 mph (277 km/h), (TOW configuration), 141 mph (227 km/h); max inclined climb, 1,620 ft/min (8,23 m/sec); hovering ceiling TOW configuration (in ground effect), 12,200 ft (3 720 m); max range, 357 mls (574 km).
Weights: (TOW configuration). Operational empty, 6,479 lb (2 939 kg); max take-off, 10,000 lb (4 535 kg).
Dimensions: Rotor diam, 44 ft 0 in (13,41 m); fuselage length, 44 ft 7 in (13,59 m).
Notes: The AH-1S is a dedicated attack and anti-armour helicopter serving primarily with the US Army which had received 297 new-production AH-1S HueyCobras by mid-1982, plus 290 resulting from the conversion of earlier AH-1G and AH-1Q HueyCobras. Current planning calls for conversion of a further 372 AH-1Gs to AH-1S standards, and both conversion and new-production AH-1S HueyCobras have been progressively upgraded to 'Modernised AH-1S' standard, the entire programme having been completed in 1985, resulting in a total of 959 'Modernised' AH-1S HueyCobras. The AH-1S is being licence-built in Japan by Fuji for the Ground Self-Defence Force which has received 54 examples, and the AH-1S has also been supplied to Jordan, Israel and Pakistan (a Pakistan example being illustrated above).

BELL AH-1W SUPERCOBRA

Country of Origin: USA.
Type: Two-seat light attack helicopter.
Power Plant: Two 1,693 shp General Electric T700-GE-401 turboshafts.
Performance: Max cruising speed, 184 mph (296 km/h) at 3,000 ft (915 m); hovering ceiling (out of ground effect), 10,000 ft (3 050 m); range, 380 mls (611 km) at 3,000 ft (915 m).
Weights: Empty, 9,700 lb (4 400 kg); max take-off, 14,750 lb (6 691 kg).
Dimensions: Rotor diam, 48 ft 0 in (14,63 m); fuselage length, 45 ft 3 in (13,79 m).
Notes: Flown for the first time on 16 November 1983, the AH-1W SuperCobra is an enhanced-capability derivative of the AH-1T SeaCobra (see 1984 edition) of the US Marine Corps. The first of an initial batch of 22 SuperCobras was delivered to the USMC in March 1986, and a follow-on batch of a further 22 was ordered September 1985. Current USMC planning calls for modification of 44 AH-1Ts to -1W standard and procurement of 34 more newbuild -1Ws from Fiscal 1987 funding. More powerful and more heavily armed than the SeaCobra, the primary USMC mission of the SuperCobra will be to provide escort for troop-carrying helicopters, and in this role it can augment its 20-mm three-barrel rotary cannon with up to four AIM-9L Sidewinder missiles on the stub-wing pylons. A typical load for the anti-armour mission can comprise eight laser-guided Hellfire launch-and-leave missiles.

BELL MODEL 214ST

Country of Origin: USA.
Type: Medium transport helicopter (20 seats).
Power Plant: Two 1,625 shp (limited to combined output of 2,250 shp) General Electric CT7-2A turboshafts.
Performance: Max cruising speed, 164 mph (264 km/h) at sea level, 161 mph (259 km/h) at 4,000 ft (1 220 m); hovering ceiling (in ground effect), 12,600 ft (3 840 m), (out of ground effect), 3,300 ft (1 005 m); range (standard fuel), 460 mls (740 km).
Weights: Max take-off (internal or external load), 17,500 lb (7 938 kg).
Dimensions: Rotor diam, 52 ft 0 in (15,85 m); fuselage length, 50 ft 0 in (15,24 m).
Notes: The Model 214ST (Super Transport) is a significantly improved derivative of the Model 214B BigLifter (see 1978 edition), production of which was phased out early 1981, initial customer deliveries of the Model 214ST beginning early 1982. The Model 214ST test-bed was first flown in March 1977, and the first of three representative prototypes (one in military configuration and two for commercial certification) commenced its test programme in August 1979. Work on an initial series of 100 helicopters of this type commenced in 1981. A version with wheel landing gear was certificated in March 1983, and alternative layouts are available for either 16 or 17 passengers. Military operators include the Venezuelan and Peruvian air forces, and the Royal Thai Army.

BELL MODEL 222B

Country of Origin: USA.
Type: Eight/ten-seat light utility and transport helicopter.
Power Plant: Two 680 shp Textron Lycoming LTS 101-750C-1 turboshafts.
Performance: Max cruising speed, 150 mph (241 km/h) at sea level, 146 mph (235 km/h) at 8,000 ft (2 400 m); max climb, 1,730 ft/min (8,8 m/sec); hovering ceiling (in ground effect), 10,300 ft (3 135 m), (out of ground effect), 6,400 ft (1 940 m); range (no reserves), 450 mls (724 km) at 8,000 ft (2 400 m).
Weights: Empty equipped, 4,577 lb (2 076 kg); max take-off (standard configuration), 8,250 lb (3 742 kg).
Dimensions: Rotor diam, 42 ft 0 in (12,80 m); fuselage length, 39 ft 9 in (12,12 m).
Notes: The first of five prototypes of the Model 222 was flown on 13 August 1976, an initial production series of 250 helicopters of this type being initiated in 1978, with production deliveries commencing in January 1980, and some 200 delivered by beginning of 1988, when production rate was one monthly. Several versions of the Model 222 are on offer or under development, these including an executive version with a flight crew of two and five or six passengers, and the so-called 'offshore' model with accommodation for eight passengers and a flight crew of two. The Model 222B has a larger main rotor and uprated power plant, a utility version, the Model 222UT (illustrated), having been certificated mid 1983, with deliveries commencing shortly afterwards.

BELL MODEL 412

Country of Origin: USA.
Type: Fifteen-seat utility transport helicopter.
Power Plant: One 1,800 shp Pratt & Whitney PT6T-3B-1 turboshaft.
Performance: Max speed, 149 mph (240 km/h) at sea level; cruise, 143 mph (230 km/h) at sea level, 146 mph (235 km/h) at 5,000 ft (1 525 m); hovering ceiling (in ground effect), 10,800 ft (3 290 m), (out of ground effect), 7,100 ft (2 165 m) at 10,500 lb/4 763 kg; max range, 282 mls (454 km), (with auxiliary tanks), 518 mls (834 km).
Weights: Empty equipped, 6,535 lb (2 964 kg); max take-off, 11,900 lb (5 397 kg).
Dimensions: Rotor diam, 46 ft 0 in (14,02 m); fuselage length, 41 ft 8½ in (12,70 m).
Notes: The Model 412, flown for the first time in August 1979, is an updated Model 212 (production of which was continuing at the beginning of 1988) with a new-design four-bladed rotor, a shorter rotor mast assembly, and uprated engine and transmission systems, giving more than twice the life of the Model 212 units. Composite rotor blades are used and the rotor head incorporates elastomeric bearings and dampers to simplify moving parts. An initial series of 200 helicopters was laid down with customer deliveries commencing February 1981. Licence manufacture is undertaken by Agusta in Italy, a multi-purpose military version being designated AB 412 Griffon, and production is also being undertaken by IPTN in Indonesia.

BOEING 414 CHINOOK

Country of Origin: USA.
Type: Medium transport helicopter.
Power Plant: Two 3,750 shp Textron Lycoming T55-L-712 turboshafts.
Performance: (At 45,400 lb/20 593 kg) Max speed, 146 mph (235 km/h) at sea level; average cruise, 131 mph (211 km/h); max inclined climb, 1,380 ft/min (7,0 m/sec); service ceiling, 8,400 ft (2 560 m); max ferry range, 1,190 mls (1 915 km).
Weights: Empty, 22,591 lb (10 247 kg); max take-off, 50,000 lb (22 680 kg).
Dimensions: Rotor diam (each), 60 ft 0 in (18,29 m); fuselage length, 51 ft 0 in (15.55 m).
Notes: The Model 414 as supplied to the RAF as the Chinook HC Mk 1 combines some features of the US Army's CH-47D (see 1980 edition) and features of the Canadian CH-147, but with provision for glassfibre/carbonfibre rotor blades. The first of 33 Chinook HC Mk 1s for the RAF was flown on 23 March 1980 and accepted on 2 December 1980, with deliveries continuing through 1981, three more being ordered in 1982 and five in 1983. The RAF version can accommodate 44 troops and has three external cargo hooks. During 1981, Boeing Vertol initiated the conversion to essentially similar CH-47D standards a total of 436 CH-47As, Bs and Cs, and this programme is scheduled for completion in 1993. More than 100 Model 414s have been built by Agusta, and 52 are being co-produced by Kawasaki in Japan.

EH INDUSTRIES EH 101

Countries of Origin: United Kingdom and Italy.
Type: Shipboard anti-submarine warfare, military and commercial transport and utility helicopter.
Power Plant: Three (naval version) 1,729 shp General Electric CT7-2A or (civil and utility) 2,000 shp CT7-6 turboshafts.
Performance: Typical cruise speed, 173 mph (278 km/h); hovering ceiling (IGE), 9,000 ft (2 745 m), (OGE) 5,500 ft (1 675 m); range (utility version with 7,000-lb/3 175-kg payload), 402 mls (648 km).
Weights: Operational empty (naval version), 20,448 lb (9 725 kg), (civil transport), 18,876 lb (8 562 kg); max take-off (naval version), 28,660 lb (13 000 kg), (civil transport), 31,500 lb (14 290 kg).
Dimensions: Rotor diam, 61 ft 0 in (18,59 m); overall length (rotors turning), 75 ft 3 in (22,94 m).
Notes: EH Industries comprises Westland Helicopters of the UK and Agusta of Italy, the company having been formed specifically for the development of the multi-role EH 101, the first of nine development examples of which flew (in the UK) on 9 October and the second (in Italy) on 14 December 1987. The fourth and fifth EH 101s will be naval prototypes, the sixth an army utility prototype, and the eighth and ninth will be civil prototypes. The civil transport will accommodate 30 passengers four abreast and the army utility version will carry up to 28 combat-equipped troops. Certification of the basic EH 101 is scheduled for September 1990.

KAMOV KA-27 (HELIX)

Country of Origin: USSR.
Type: (Ka-27) Shipboard anti-submarine warfare and (Ka-32) utility transport helicopter.
Power Plant: Two 2,205 shp Isotov TV3-117V turboshafts.
Performance: (Ka-32) Max speed, 155 mph (250 km/h); max continuous cruise, 143 mph (230 km/h); max range, 497 mls (800 km); service ceiling (at 24,250 lb/11 000 kg), 16,405 ft (5 000 m).
Weights: (Ka-32) Normal loaded, 24,250 lb (11 000 kg); max loaded (with external load), 27,778 lb (12 600 kg).
Dimensions: Rotor diam (each), 52 ft 1⅞ in (15,90 m); overall length, 37 ft 0⅞ in (11,30 m).
Notes: Believed to have flown in prototype form in 1979–80, and first seen in ASW Ka-27 form during Zapad-81 exercises in the Baltic in September 1981, this Kamov helicopter has also been developed for civil roles as the Ka-32, variants including a dedicated search-and-rescue variant, the Ka-32S. The naval Ka-27 and civil Ka-32 appear to differ in no fundamental respect apart from equipment, and the former is now the standard equipment aboard carriers of the Soviet Navy in basic ASW Helix-A form and in Helix-B form for missile target acquisition and mid-course guidance. The Ka-32S is capable of adverse weather and day or night operation, and is equipped with a 661-lb (300-kg) capacity winch for the ASR role. A slung load of up to five *tonnes* (11,023 lb can be lifted by this version). The Helix-C (illustrated) is a SAR and plane guard version.

KAMOV (HOKUM)

Country of Origin: USSR.
Type: Tandem two-seat combat helicopter.
Power Plant: Two unidentified turboshafts (possibly related to Isotov TV3-117).
Performance: (Estimated) Max speed, 217 mph (350 km/h); combat radius, 155 mls (250 km).
Weights: (Estimated) Normal loaded, 12,000 lb (5 450 kg).
Dimensions: (Estimated) Rotor diam (each), 59 ft 8 in (18,20 m); length (overall), 52 ft 6 in (16,00 m); height, 17 ft 8 in (5,40 m).
Notes: Possibly the first true air-to-air combat helicopter, intended to eliminate opposing frontline helicopters and presumably featuring a secondary close support role, the Hokum currently possesses no western counterpart. Flight testing of this helicopter is believed to have commenced late 1983 or early 1984, and initial operational capability is anticipated 1988–89. The accompanying illustration should be considered as provisional, but is based on the latest available information and depicts the general configuration. Retaining the superimposed co-axial rotor arrangement which has become the trademark of the Kamov bureau, this dedicated combat helicopter is believed to include a fixed heavy-calibre gun in its armament, underwing pylons being provided for tube-launched missiles for air–air or air–ground use, or anti-armour missiles. Western analysts believe that introduction of Hokum will provide a significant helicopter air superiority capability.

MBB BO 105LS

Country of Origin: Federal Germany.
Type: Five/six-seat light utility helicopter.
Power Plant: Two 550 shp Allison 250-C28C turboshafts.
Performance: Max speed, 168 mph (270 km/h) at sea level; max cruise, 157 mph (252 km/h) at sea level; max climb, 1,970 ft/min (10 m/sec); hovering ceiling (in ground effect), 13,120 ft (4 000 m), (out of ground effect), 11,280 ft (3 440 m); range, 286 mls (460 km).
Weights: Empty, 2,756 lb (1 250 kg); max take-off, 5,291 lb (2 400 kg), (with external load), 5,512 lb (2 500 kg).
Dimensions: Rotor diam, 32 ft 3½ in (9,84 m); fuselage length, 28 ft 1 in (8,56 m).
Notes: The BO 105LS is a derivative of the BO 105CB (see 1979 edition) with uprated transmission and more powerful turboshaft for 'hot-and-high' conditions. It is otherwise similar to the BO 105CBS Twin Jet II (420 shp Allison 250-C20B) which was continuing in production at the beginning of 1988, when more than 1,200 BO 105s (all versions) had been delivered, production was running at five monthly, and licence assembly has been undertaken in Indonesia, the Philippines and Spain. Deliveries to the Federal German Army of 227 BP 105M helicopters for liaison and observation tasks commenced late 1979, and deliveries of 212 HOT-equipped BO 105Ps for the anti-armour role began on 4 December 1980 and were completed mid-1984. The latter have uprated engines and transmission systems.

MBB-KAWASAKI BK 117 A-3

Countries of Origin: Federal Germany and Japan.
Type: Multi-purpose eight-to-twelve-seat helicopter.
Power Plant: Two 600 shp Textron Lycoming LTS 101-650B1 or 750 shp-750B1 turboshafts.
Performance: Max speed, 171 mph (275 km/h) at sea level; cruise, 164 mph (264 km/h) at sea level; max climb, 1,970 ft/min (10 m/sec); hovering ceiling (in ground effect), 13,450 ft (4 100 m), (out of ground effect), 10,340 ft (3 150 m); range (max payload), 339 mls (545 km).
Weights: Empty, 3,351 lb (1 520 kg); max take-off, 6,173 lb (2 800 kg).
Dimensions: Rotor diam, 36 ft 1 in (11,00 m); fuselage length, 32 ft 5 in (9,88 m).
Notes: The BK 117 is a co-operative development between Messerschmitt-Bölkow-Blohm and Kawasaki, the first of two flying prototypes commencing its flight test programme on 13 June 1979 (in Germany), with the second following on 10 August (in Japan). A decision to proceed with series production was taken in 1980, with first flying on 24 December 1981, and production deliveries commencing first quarter of 1983 in which year 20 were delivered. A further 20 were built in 1984, and production tempo was two monthly at the beginning of 1988. MBB is responsible for the main and tail rotor systems, tail unit and hydraulic components, while Kawasaki is responsible for the fuselage, undercarriage and transmission. The BK 117 A-3M is a purely German multi-role military version.

McDONNELL DOUGLAS 500MD DEFENDER II

Country of Origin: USA.
Type: Light gunship and multi-role helicopter.
Power Plant: One 420 shp Allison 250-C20B turboshaft.
Performance: (At 3,000 lb/1 362 kg) Max speed, 175 mph (282 km/h) at sea level; cruise, 160 mph (257 km/h) at 4,000 ft (1 220 m); max inclined climb, 1,920 ft/min (9,75 m/sec); hovering ceiling (in ground effect), 8,800 ft (2 682 m), (out of ground effect), 7,100 ft (2 164 m); max range, 263 mls (423 km).
Weights: Empty, 1,295 lb (588 kg); max take-off (internal load), 3,000 lb (1 362 kg), (with external load), 3,620 lb (1 642 kg).
Dimensions: Rotor diam, 26 ft 5 in (8,05 m); fuselage length, 21 ft 5 in (6,52 m).
Notes: The Defender II multi-mission version of the Model 500MD was introduced mid-1980 for 1982 delivery, and features a Martin Marietta rotor mast-top sight, a General Dynamics twin-Stinger air-to-air missile pod, an underfuselage 30-mm chain gun and a pilot's night vision sensor. The Defender II can be rapidly reconfigured for anti-armour target designation, anti-helicopter, suppressive fire and transport roles. The Model 500MD TOW Defender (carrying four tube-launched optically-tracked wire-guided anti-armour missiles) is currently in service with Israel (30), South Korea (45) and Kenya (15). Production of the 500 was seven monthly at the beginning of 1988, when upgraded versions, Model 500ME, and MG Paramilitary Defender, were offered.

McDONNELL DOUGLAS 530F LIFTER

Country of Origin: USA.

Type: Five-seat light utility helicopter.

Power Plant: One 650 shp Allison 250-C30 turboshaft.

Performance: Max cruise speed, 155 mph (250 km/h) at sea level, econ cruise, 150 mph (241 km/h) at 5,000 ft (1 525 m); max inclined climb, 1,780 ft/min (9,04 m/sec); hovering ceiling (in ground effect), 12,000 ft (3 660 m), (out of ground effect), 9,600 ft (2 925 m); range, 269 mls (434 km) at 5,000 ft (1 525 m).

Weights: Max take-off, 3,100 lb (1 406 kg).

Dimensions: Rotor diam, 27 ft 6 in (8,38 m); fuselage length, 23 ft 2½ in (7,07 m).

Notes: The Model 530F is the 'hot and high' variant of the Model 500E (see 1983 edition under Hughes 500E) which is characterised by a longer, recontoured nose compared with the preceding Model 500D, offering increased leg room for front seat occupants and a 12 per cent increase in headroom for rear seat passengers. The principal differences between the Models 500E and 530F are the larger diameter rotors and the power plant, the former having a 520 shp 250-C20B. The Model 500E was flown on 28 January 1982, and was certificated in November 1982, and the Model 530F was flown in October 1982. Customer deliveries of the Model 530F began in January 1984, and on the following 4 May a military version, the Model 530MG, entered flight test, this being intended primarily for the light attack mission and being essentially similar to the 500ME apart from power plant.

McDONNELL DOUGLAS AH-64 APACHE

Country of Origin: USA.

Type: Tandem two-seat attack helicopter.

Power Plant: Two 1,690 shp General Electric T700-GE-701 turboshafts.

Performance: Max speed, 191 mph (307 km/h); cruise, 179 mph (288 km/h); max inclined climb, 3,200 ft/min (16,27 m/sec); hovering ceiling (in ground effect), 14,600 ft (4 453 m), (out of ground effect), 11,800 ft (3 600 m); service ceiling, 21,000 ft (6 400 m); max range, 424 mls (682 km).

Weights: Empty, 9,900 lb (4 490 kg); primary mission, 13,600 lb (6 169 kg); max take-off, 17,400 lb (7 892 kg).

Dimensions: Rotor diam, 48 ft 0 in (14,63 m); fuselage length, 48 ft 1$\frac{7}{8}$ in (14,70 m).

Notes: Winning contender in the US Army's AAH (Advanced Attack Helicopter) contest, the AH-64 flew for the first time on 30 September 1975. Two prototypes were used for the initial trials, the first of three more with fully integrated weapons systems commenced trials on 31 October 1979, a further three following in 1980. Planned total procurement comprises 675 AH-64s through 1990, with 593 ordered by beginning of 1987, and a production rate of 10 monthly, deliveries having commenced during the summer of 1984 with a total of 310 having been delivered by the beginning of 1988. The AH-64 is armed with a single-barrel 30-mm gun based on the chain-driven bolt system and suspended beneath the fuselage, and eight BGM-71A TOW or 16 Hellfire missiles may be carried.

MIL MI-8/17 (HIP)

Country of Origin: USSR.
Type: Assault transport helicopter.
Power Plant: Two (Mi-8) 1,700 shp Isotov TV2-117A or (Mi-17) 1,900 shp TV3-117MT turboshafts.
Performance: Max speed (Mi-8 at 26,455 lb/12 000 kg), 142 mph (230 km/h), (Mi-17 at 28,660 lb/13 000 kg), 155 mph (250 km/h); max cruise (Mi-8), 112 mph (180 km/h), (Mi-17) 149 mph (240 km/h); hovering ceiling (Mi-8 at 24,470 lb/11 100 kg in ground effect), 6,235 ft (1 900 m), (out of ground effect), 2,625 ft (800 m), (Mi-17 at 24,470 lb/11 100 kg out of ground effect), 5,775 ft (1 760 m).
Weights: Empty equipped (typical), 16,000 lb (7 260 kg); max take-off (Mi-8), 26,455 lb (12 000 kg), (Mi-17) 26,660 lb (13 000 kg).
Dimensions: Rotor diam, 69 ft $10\frac{1}{4}$ in (21,29 m); fuselage length (Mi-8), 59 ft $7\frac{3}{8}$ in (18,17 m), (Mi-17) 60 ft $5\frac{5}{8}$ in (18,42 m).
Notes: The Mi-8 and Mi-17 (illustrated above) are fundamentally similar apart from power plant, both providing for a crew of three and 28 passengers in civil versions or 24 passengers on tip-up seats along sidewalls. The first prototype Mi-8 was flown in 1961, series production (Hip-C) commencing in 1963, with more than 10,000 (all versions) since delivered and manufacture continuing (of Mi-17) at a rate of 700 annually. Military versions include the Hip-C and (Mi-17) -H assault transports, the communications Hip-D and -G, and the armed Hip-E and -F. The Mi-8/17 serves with some 40 air forces.

MIL MI-24 (HIND-D)

Country of Origin: USSR.

Type: Assault and anti-armour helicopter.

Power Plant: Two 2,200 shp Isotov TV3-117 turboshafts.

Performance: (Estimated) Max speed, 170–180 mph (273–290 km/h) at 3,280 ft (1 000 m); max cruise, 145 mph (233 km/h); max inclined climb rate, 3,000 ft/min (15 24 m/sec).

Weights: (Estimated) Normal take-off (with four missiles), 22,000 lb (10 000 kg).

Dimensions: (Estimated) Rotor diam, 55 ft 0 in (16,76 m); fuselage length, 55 ft 6 in (16,90 m).

Notes: By comparison with the Hind-A version of the Mi-24 (see 1977 edition), the Hind-D embodies a redesigned forward fuselage and is optimised for the gunship role, having tandem stations for the weapons operator (in nose) and pilot. The Hind-D can accommodate eight fully-equipped troops, has a barbette-mounted four barrel rotary-type 12,7-mm cannon beneath the nose and can carry up to 2,800 lb (1 275 kg) of ordnance externally, including four AT-2 Swatter IR-homing anti-armour missiles and four pods each with 32 57-mm rockets. It has been exported to Afghanistan, Algeria, Bulgaria, Cuba, Czechoslovakia, East Germany, Hungary, India, Iraq, Libya, Nicaragua, Poland and South Yemen. The Hind-E is similar but has provision for four laser-homing tube-launched Spiral anti-armour missiles. With the nose gun barbette deleted and replaced by a twin-barrel 30-mm cannon on the starboard fuselage side it is known as Hind-F.

MIL MI-26 (HALO)

Country of Origin: USSR.

Type: Military and commercial heavy-lift helicopter.

Power Plant: Two 11,400 shp Lotarev D-136 turboshafts.

Performance: Max speed, 183 mph (295 km/h); normal cruise, 158 mph (255 km/h); hovering ceiling (in ground effect), 14,765 ft (4 500 m), (out of ground effect), 5,905 ft (1 800 m); range (at 109,127 lb/49 500 kg), 310 mls (500 km), (at 123,457 lb/ 56 000 kg), 497 mls (800 km).

Weights: Empty, 62,169 lb (28 200 kg); normal loaded, 109,227 lb (49 500 kg); max take-off, 123,457 lb (56 000 kg).

Dimensions: Rotor diam, 104 ft 11$\frac{7}{8}$ in (32,00 m); fuselage length (nose to tail rotor), 110 ft 7$\frac{3}{4}$ in (33,73 m).

Notes: The heaviest and most powerful helicopter ever flown, the Mi-26 first flew as a prototype on 14 December 1977, production of pre-series machines commencing in 1980, and preparations for full-scale production having begun in 1981. Featuring an innovative eight-bladed main rotor and carrying a flight crew of five, the Mi-26 has a max internal payload of 44,090 lb (20 000 kg). The freight hold is larger than that of the fixed-wing Antonov An-12 transport and at least 70 combat-equipped troops or 40 casualty stretchers can be accommodated. Although allegedly developed to a civil requirement, the primary role of the Mi-26 is obviously military and the Soviet Air Force achieved initial operational capability with the series version late 1983. Ten Mi-26 helicopters have been supplied to India (as illustrated).

MIL MI-28 (HAVOC)

Country of Origin: USSR.
Type: Tandem two-seat attack helicopter.
Power Plant: Two 2,000–2,500 shp turboshafts (possibly related to the Isotov TV3-117).
Performance: (Estimated) Max speed, 186 mph (300 km/h); tactical radius, 149 mls (240 km).
Weights: No details available for publication.
Dimensions: (Estimated) Rotor diam, 55 ft 9 in (17,00 m); fuselage length (including tail rotor), 57 ft 1 in (17,40 m).
Notes: Development of the Mi-28 (the above illustration of which should be considered as provisional) is believed to have commenced in the early 'eighties, and it is expected to be deployed by attack helicopter regiments during the course of 1988. The Mi-28 has a single large-calibre gun (probably a multi-barrel 23-mm weapon) in an undernose barbette, and pylons beneath each stub wing are expected to carry pods each containing four laser-guided anti-armour missiles, plus tube-launched missiles for air–air or air–ground use at their tips. The Mi-28 is closely comparable in size and performance capability with the AH-64 Apache, and, unlike the Mi-24 (Hind), possesses no transport capability, design emphasis having apparently been placed on agility and survivability. The structure is believed to embody integral armour around the area of the tandem cockpits, and noteworthy features include the pod-mounted engines with upward deflected jet pipes. The Mi-28 is equipped with infra-red suppressors and infra-red decoy dispensers.

SIKORSKY CH-53E SUPER STALLION

Country of Origin: USA.

Type: Amphibious assault transport helicopter.

Power Plant: Three 4,380 shp General Electric T64-GE-415 turboshafts.

Performance: (At 56,000 lb/25 400 kg) Max speed, 196 mph (315 km/h) at sea level; cruise, 173 mph (278 km/h) at sea level; max inclined climb, 2,750 ft/min (13,97 m/sec); hovering ceiling (in ground effect), 11,550 ft (3 520 m), (out of ground effect), 9,500 ft (2 895 m); 1,290 mls (2 075 km).

Weights: Empty, 33,226 lb (15 071 kg); max take-off, 73,500 lb (33 339 kg).

Dimensions: Rotor diam, 79 ft 0 in (24,08 m); fuselage length, 73 ft 5 in (22,38 m).

Notes: The CH-53E is a growth version of the CH-53D Sea Stallion (see 1974 edition) embodying a third engine, an uprated transmission system, a seventh main rotor blade and increased rotor diameter. The first of two prototypes was flown on 1 March 1974, and the first of two pre-production examples followed on 8 December 1975, production of two per month being divided between the US Navy and US Marine Corps at beginning of 1988, against total requirement for 160 through 1992. The CH-53E can accommodate up to 55 troops in a high-density seating arrangement. Fleet deliveries began mid-1981, and the first production example of the MH-53E Sea Dragon (illustrated) mine countermeasures version (35 required by US Navy) was delivered in June 1986.

SIKORSKY S-70 (UH-60A) BLACK HAWK

Country of Origin: USA.
Type: Tactical transport helicopter.
Power Plant: Two 1,543 shp General Electric T700-GE-700 turboshafts.
Performance: Max speed, 224 mph (360 km/h) at sea level; cruise, 166 mph (267 km/h); vertical climb rate, 450 ft/min (2,28 m/sec); hovering ceiling (in ground effect), 10,000 ft (3 048 m), (out of ground effect), 5,800 ft (1 758 m); endurance, 2·3–3·0 hrs.
Weights: Design gross, 16,500 lb (7 485 kg); max take-off, 22,000 lb (9 979 kg).
Dimensions: Rotor diam, 53 ft 8 in (16,23 m); fuselage length, 50 ft 0¾ in (15,26 m).
Notes: The Black Hawk was winner of the US Army's UTTAS (Utility Tactical Transport Aircraft System) contest. The first of three YUH-60As was flown on 17 October 1974, and a company-funded fourth prototype flew on 23 May 1975. The Black Hawk is primarily a combat assault squad carrier, accommodating 11 fully-equipped troops. Variants include the EH-60A ECM model, deliveries of which commenced late 1985, and the HH-60A Night Hawk rescue helicopter. The USAF is expected to procure 90 HH-60s and 77 EH-60s. The first production deliveries of the UH-60A to the US Army were made in June 1979, with some 900 delivered by beginning of 1988 against requirement for 1,107. The RAAF ordered 39 (against requirement for 48) of the S-70A-9 export Black Hawk during 1986–7.

SIKORSKY S-70L (SH-60B) SEA HAWK

Country of Origin: USA.
Type: Shipboard multi-role helicopter.
Power Plant: Two 1,690 shp General Electric T700-GE-401 turboshafts.
Performance: (At 20,244 lb/9 183 kg) Max speed, 167 mph (269 km/h) at sea level; max cruising speed, 155 mph (249 km/h) at 5,000 ft (1 525 m); max vertical climb, 1,192 ft/min (6,05 m/sec); time on station (at radius of 57 mls/92 km), 3 hrs 52 min.
Weights: Empty equipped, 13,678 lb (6 204 kg); max take-off, 21,844 lb (9 908 kg).
Dimensions: Rotor diam, 53 ft 8 in (16,36 m); fuselage length, 50 ft 0¾ in (15,26 m).
Notes: Winner of the US Navy's LAMPS (Light Airborne Multi-Purpose System) Mk III helicopter contest, the SH-60B is intended to fulfil both anti-submarine warfare (ASW) and anti-ship surveillance and targeting (ASST) missions, and the first of five prototypes was flown on 12 December 1979, and the last on 14 July 1980. Evolved from the UH-60A (see page 246), the SH-60B is intended to serve aboard DD-963 destroyers, DDG-47 Aegis cruisers and FFG-7 guided missile frigates as an integral extension of the sensor and weapon system of the launching vessel. The US Navy has a requirement for 204 SH-60Bs, the first of which was delivered in October 1983, and for 175 simplified SH-60Fs without MAD gear. The Australian Navy has ordered 16 Sea Hawks with deliveries commencing 1988, the first having flown on 4 December 1987.

SIKORSKY S-70C

Country of Origin: USA.
Type: Commercial transport helicopter.
Power Plant: Two 1,625 shp General Electric CT7-2C turbo-shafts.
Performance: Econ cruise speed, 186 mph (300 km/h); max inclined climb rate, 2,770 ft/min (14,1 m/sec); service ceiling, 17,200 ft (5,240 m); hovering ceiling (in ground effect), 8,700 ft (2 650 m), (out of ground effect), 4,800 ft (1 460 m); range (standard fuel with reserves), 294 mls (473 km) at 155 mph (250 km/h) at 3,000 ft (915 m), (max fuel without reserves), 342 mls (550 km).
Weights: Empty, 10,158 lb (4 607 kg); max take-off, 20,250 lb (9 185 kg).
Dimensions: Rotor diam, 53 ft 8 in (16,36 m); fuselage length, 50 ft 0¾ in (15,26 m).
Notes: The S-70C is a commercial derivative of the H-60 series of military helicopters, and may be configured for a variety of utility missions, such as maritime and environmental survey, mineral exploration and external lift, provision being made for an 8,000-lb (3 629-kg) capacity external cargo hook. Options include a winterisation kit, a cabin-mounted rescue hoist and an aeromedical evacuation kit. The S-70C has a flight deck crew of two and can accommodate 12 passengers in standard cabin configuration or up to 19 passengers in high density layout. Twenty-four were delivered to China during 1985, and 14 were ordered during 1986 by the Nationalist Chinese Air Force.

SIKORSKY S-76B

Country of Origin: USA.

Type: Commercial transport helicopter.

Power Plant: Two 960 shp Pratt & Whitney (Canada) PT6B-36 turboshafts.

Performance: Max cruise speed, 167 mph (269 km/h); econ cruise, 155 mph (250 km/h); max inclined climb, 1,700 ft/min (8,63 m/sec); service ceiling, 16,000 ft (4 875 m); hovering ceiling (in ground effect), 8,700 ft (2 650 m), (out of ground effect), 5,900 ft (1 800 m); range (max payload), 207 mls (333 km), (max standard fuel), 414 mls (667 km).

Weights: Empty, 6,250 lb (2 835 kg); max take-off, 11,000 lb (4 989 kg).

Dimensions: Rotor diam, 44 ft 0 in (13,41 m); fuselage length, 43 ft 4½ in (13,22 m).

Notes: The S-76B is a derivative of the S-76 Mk II (see 1984 edition) from which it differs primarily in the type of power plant. A prototype of the S-76B was flown for the first time on 22 June 1984, and first customer deliveries were effected the first half of 1985. Offering a 51 per cent increase in useful load under hot and high conditions by comparison with the S-76 Mk II, the S-76B provides accommodation for a flight crew of two and a maximum of 12 passengers. A total of some 300 S-76 helicopters (all versions) had been delivered by the beginning of 1988, including more than 30 S-76Bs. Commercial and military utility versions (see page 250) are available, a multi-role naval version, the H-76N, being under development.

SIKORSKY H-76 EAGLE

Country of Origin: USA.
Type: Armed light utility helicopter.
Power Plant: Two 960 shp Pratt & Whitney (Canada) PT6B-36 turboshafts.
Performance: Max cruise speed, 165 mph (265 km/h); econ cruise, 150 mph (241 km/h); max inclined climb, 1,650 ft/min (8,38 m/sec); service ceiling, 16,000 ft (4 875 m); hovering ceiling (in ground effect), 8,800 ft (2 682 m), (out of ground effect), 5,900 ft (1 800 m); range (standard fuel), 360 mls (578 km) with 30 min reserves.
Weights: Empty equipped (typical), 6,680 lb (3 030 kg); max take-off, 11,400 lb (5 171 kg).
Dimensions: Rotor diam, 44 ft 0 in (13,41 m); fuselage length, 43 ft 4½ in (13,22 m).
Notes: The H-76 Eagle is a military derivative of the S-76B and was first flown in February 1985. Intended to fulfil attack, combat support, troop transportation, medevac and SAR missions, and capable of being reconfigured for different roles within 30 min, the H-76 incorporates optional armoured crew seats, sliding doors and a heavy duty floor. A wide range of optional items, including weapon pylons, self-sealing high-strength fuel tanks and provision for door-mounted weapons, is offered, and equipped for transportation up to 10 fully-equipped troops may be accommodated. The standard medevac layout provides for three casualty litters and two medical attendants.

WESTLAND SUPER LYNX

Country of Origin: United Kingdom.
Type: Multi-role maritime helicopter.
Power Plant: Two 1,120 shp Rolls-Royce Gem 42 turboshafts.
Performance: Max continuous cruise speed, 161 mph (260 km/h) at sea level; normal inclined climb, 1,970 ft/min (10 m/sec); range (anti-surface vessel role with four ASMs and 20 min reserves), 265 mls (426 km), (search and rescue), 391 mls (630 km).
Weights: Max take-off, 11,300 lb (5 126 kg).
Dimensions: Rotor diam, 42 ft 0 in (12,80 m); length (main rotor folded), 45 ft 3 in (13,79 m).
Notes: Under development at the beginning of 1987 with availability from late 1988, the Super Lynx is the latest development of the Lynx family and is intended to fulfil anti-shipping, anti-submarine and search and rescue roles. The principal new features by comparison with earlier naval Lynx helicopters include a MEL Super Searcher 360 deg radar installation, increased fuel capacity and a redesigned tail rotor. Provision is made to carry up to four Sea Skua, AS 12 or AS 15TT air-to-surface missiles or two long-range Penguin missiles, and in the rescue role the cabin can accommodate eight survivors, or, more typically, three stretcher cases and a medical attendant. Radius of action with three crew, a 600-lb (272-kg) capacity hoist and six survivors is 174 mls (280 km). A total of 342 of the earlier Lynx had been ordered by the beginning of 1988.

WESTLAND SEA KING

Country of Origin: United Kingdom (US licence).

Type: Anti-submarine warfare and search-and-rescue helicopter.

Power Plant: Two 1,465 shp Rolls-Royce Gnome H.1400-1T turboshafts.

Performance: Max speed, 143 mph (230 km/h); max continuous cruise at sea level, 131 mph (211 km/h); hovering ceiling (in ground effect), 5,000 ft (1 525 m), (out of ground effect), 3,200 ft (975 m); range (standard fuel), 764 mls (1 230 km), (auxiliary fuel), 937 mls (1 507 km).

Weights: Empty equipped (ASW), 13,672 lb (6 201 kg), (SAR), 12,376 lb (5 613 kg); max take-off, 21,500 lb (9 752 kg).

Dimensions: Rotor diam, 62 ft 0 in (18,90 m); fuselage length, 55 ft 9¾ in (17,01 m).

Notes: The Sea King Mk 2 is an uprated version of the basic ASW and SAR derivative of the licence-built S-61D (see 1982 edition), the first Mk 2 being flown on 30 June 1974, and being one of 10 Sea King Mk 50s ordered by the Australian Navy. Twenty-one to the Royal Navy as HAS Mk 2s, and 19 examples of a SAR version to the RAF as HAR Mk 3s. Current production version is the HAS Mk 6, to be delivered to the Royal Navy from November 1989 onwards. All HAS Mk 2s brought up to Mk 5 standards and eight Mks 2 and 3 fitted with Thorn-EMI searchwater radar for airborne early warning duty. Westland Sea King sales 'exceeded 330' by beginning of 1988. The HAS Mk 5 is illustrated above.

INDEX OF AIRCRAFT TYPES